Whistling Sousa

A Whistling Pines mystery

Dean L Hovey

Dedicated to Frank S. Hovey
Major USMC
1920-2012

This book is a work of fiction. The events, places, and people are fictional products of the author's imagination or are used fictionally. Any resemblance to actual events is coincidental and unintended.

ISBN: 1938382048
ISBN 13: 9781938382048

Whistling Sousa

A Whistling Pines mystery

Dean L Hovey

Prologue

The four-day Lake County Fair is held each August in Two Harbors, Minnesota, near the western tip of Lake Superior. It isn't a big event in terms of acreage or even the number of attractions, but when you live in a rural Minnesota county extending from the frigid north shore of Lake Superior to the nearly-arctic Canadian border, any summer event draws huge crowds. The fair serves as the regional clearinghouse for 4H projects; the winners take their projects, whether animal or craft, to St. Paul (aka The Cities) to compete at the 10-day Minnesota State Fair. For many of the rural teens the three-hour, 180-mile drive to the State Fair is their first trip south of Duluth, and their first chance to realize there is a larger pool of future spouses than just the people they've known since kindergarten.

Fairgoers from tiny towns trust their neighbors, leave their houses unlocked, and walk the fairgrounds without a thought about crime. None suspect that a murderer is among them.

Chapter 1

Thursday

Everyone loves a day at the fair and the residents of Whistling Pines, the senior citizen assisted-living facility located in Two Harbors, are no exception, many of them having attended every county fair since childhood. The living arrangements at Whistling Pines range from apartments with meals provided to people who live independently but require assistance with their medications and personal care. The more mobile residents drive themselves and friends to the fairgrounds. Other residents are driven by friends and relatives. The rest rely on the Whistling Pines van for transportation. In my role as the Whistling Pines recreation director, I usually arrange weekly van trips for dining, shopping, and entertainment. During the third week of August I provide daily three-hour fair trips.

For the staff, the fair is one of the most trying events of the year because we have to supply one helper for every two residents who require assistance (or supervision). Lining up enough volunteers and staff to match up with pairs of residents is frustrating because any volunteer who chaperones once is unlikely to do it again. One volunteer put it best when she compared managing two retirees suffering from early Alzheimer's to herding squirrels suffering from ADHD.

On top of the logistical headaches were other challenges. The forecasted morning fog would turn into high humidity, which some residents described as soft air. If the atmospheric inversion trapped a layer of hot air over the region, others described it as a prelude to hell. One challenge is keeping our charges hydrated. Many take diuretics to treat high blood pressure and they need to drink more than the average person, followed by the need to relieve themselves proportionately, sometimes with little warning. The chaperones are coached to carry extra water bottles and are given a map so they know a direct path to the nearest restroom from any point on the fairgrounds.

The chaperones are also briefed on the dietary needs of their charges, which range from food allergies and diabetes to salt and cholesterol restrictions, which the residents often choose to ignore during a trip to the food barns where local charities cater menus of comfort food like mashed potatoes and Swedish meatballs, to calorie-laden cinnamon-and-sugar-dipped mini-doughnuts. The carnival midway is also dotted with food trailers that offer tacos, fresh-squeezed lemonade, and funnel cakes that all appeal to folks who usually eat the nutritious but repetitious and bland diet served in the Whistling Pines dining room.

The "squirrel herding" started shortly after breakfast when the residents lined up in the lobby to board the van on the first day of the fair. I checked off names from the sign-up sheet that would later help with head count when we made sure all who had been transported to the fair returned to Whistling Pines. I ticked off the names of the people in line and came up one short.

"Has anyone seen Hi Sloan this morning?" I asked, surveying the senior citizens' faces for someone to give me a credible answer.

"He was down for breakfast," a feeble female voice called from somewhere in the rear of the crowd as Wendy, the assistant director and my drafted helper for the day, pulled the small van under the front portico.

"Everyone saddle up," I told the group. "I'm running upstairs to get Hiram."

I sprinted up the stairs and jogged to Hiram's room. There wasn't a big rush, because 16 elderly people don't sprint onto a van and at least one needed to have her wheelchair loaded with the hydraulic lift. At the same time, I was concerned that something had befallen Hiram.

The muffled sounds of a television show emanated from Hiram's apartment as they did from many of the other occupied rooms, so I knocked and called his name. I heard a grumbling reply and opened the unlocked door.

Hiram was sitting in a recliner staring at the television screen and stabbing the buttons on the remote control. "Hiram," I said, "it's time to go to the fair."

He glared at me, but turned off the television. "The fair doesn't start until Thursday." He held up a calendar he kept on a small table next to his chair. Large Xs marked off the days and the last marked day was Tuesday.

"Today *is* Thursday," I said, pushing his walker in front of his chair.

"Humph," he muttered as he pushed himself to the edge of his huge recliner. "I missed a day somewhere along the line. I could've sworn it was only Wednesday."

We arrived at the van just as Jenny Chapman, the nursing supervisor and my girlfriend, helped the last of the ladies up the van steps.

"Can someone crank up the air conditioner?" a female voice asked from the rear of the van. "I'm starting to get heat stroke."

I chuckled to myself as I guided Hiram up the steps. I'd been a Navy corpsman in Iraq, and even with high humidity the Minnesota summers were cozy compared to the oven-like heat I'd experienced while serving in Iraq. I handed each of the chaperones a cloth shoulder bag embroidered with the Whistling Pines logo containing three bottles of water, and reminded them to keep their charges hydrated and to watch for signs of heat stroke.

My two "squirrels" this year were Henry "Tinker" Oldham, a one-time farmer and the town handyman, and Brad "Tubby" Nordquist, who acquired his nickname by being the fattest kid in school from first grade on. The responsibility of keeping them both in sight, while keeping them safe, hydrated, and cool was daunting. We spent half an hour walking through the 4-H handicraft displays and then exited near the livestock exhibits. I gave each of them a swig of water as we started through the cattle barn. Tinker toddled through, while Tubby lumbered along pulling his oxygen bottle, stopping at every twelve-by-twelve pen pretending to examine the cow or calf while catching his breath.

"I want to see the draft horses," Tinker said as he waited impatiently for Tubby. "When I was logging I used a team of Belgian horses to pull stumps and drag logs. Those were some fine horses. Their hooves don't break up the roots in the forest like those big skidders with caterpillar treads they use today."

As Tinker started for the horse barn I hung back and watched Tubby wipe his brow with a sodden red bandana while pretending to assess the quality of a Hereford calf that was barely a day old, tottering on untried legs and bawling for his mother. The smell of sweet fresh hay mingled with pungent manure and permeated everything. In the corner of one stall a group of teenage 4-H members were playing "Crazy Eights" using straw bales as a table and chairs.

For many of the rural kids, the county fair was *the* social event of the year, and many spent the nights catching a few hours of sleep in the stalls near their cattle while overindulging in the excitement of the competition and the fair. For some, it was the first night they'd ever spent away from parents and home. It was rumored that some experienced their first kiss at the fair, finally away from the constant supervision and work embodied by life on a farm.

Ahead of us a teenaged boy was preparing a huge Black Angus bull for judging in his pen. Although Angus cattle tend to be docile people give bulls a wide berth. Tinker, with hearing aids off to conserve their batteries and oblivious to the behemoth in the pen just ahead of him, continued walking toward the horse barn. I unsuccessfully tried to speed up Tubby. Finally dropping my bag of water and leaving him behind, I made a dash for Tinker, hoping to steer him to the far side of the aisle before he tried to pass the bull's pen. I froze in place about five feet away when Tinker, still focused on getting to the horses, reached the pen just as the behemoth suddenly started bucking like a rodeo bull. Before his young handler gained control of the animal the bull bumped against the wooden gate. I watched in horror as the gate flew open and smashed into Tinker.

By the time I got to Tinker, his eyes were rolled back and his breath was coming in short rasps. Seeing blood frothing in his mouth, I knelt by Tinker's side and ran my hands over his chest, quickly assessing his condition. Through his thin chest muscles I felt three ribs that were probably broken. The pink froth on his lips told me at least one of his ribs had punctured a lung and, depending on the severity of the injury, there was a chance he'd die, possibly before an ambulance arrived.

A quick-thinking farmer dialed 9-1-1 and within a minute a volunteer EMT, first-aid bag slung over her shoulder, came running into the barn. The young woman in a blue uniform with an EMT patch knelt next to me and I told her the patient was Henry Oldham, a resident at Whistling Pines. I gave my quick assessment of his medical condition and stepped aside so she could do her job.

I quickly checked on Tubby then watched the EMT examine Tinker for contusions and lacerations before listening to his chest. With the stethoscope still in her ears she looked at me and shook her head, which indicated his chest sounds were not good. She put an oxygen canula under his nose and turned her head to talk into a radio mic on her shoulder. I heard the words "extremely critical," the rest being lost in the cacophony around her. She held his hand and spoke softly to him until a stretcher arrived to cart Tinker to a waiting ambulance.

The Lake County Sheriff, Bill Lahti, who'd spent the day in a campaign booth shaking hands in preparation for the November election, showed up as Tubby asked me for the third time, "What happened?"

"A bull hip-checked the gate and it flew into Tinker," I explained for the third time, trying hard not to let my frustration crack through.

The sheriff was conferring with his deputies when I tapped him on the shoulder. "Excuse me. I was with the man who was injured."

The sheriff let out a sigh, put on his best campaign smile, and turned to me. "Can you hang on for a moment? I need to speak with my deputies."

"I saw the whole thing," I said. "I was trying to catch Tinker when the gate hit him."

Deputy Ron Harris, a burly middle-aged cop I'd met previously, stepped forward and directed me away from the sheriff's huddle. "I'll take your statement in a minute. Right now we're doing an accident investigation."

"Deputy Harris," I said, "I'm Peter Rogers, from Whistling Pines, the retirement community. Do you remember me from Axel Olson's murder?"

Recognition dawned on Harris's face. "Yup, you tried to keep us from looking at the crime scene. Sure, I remember you."

"The injured man is one of the Whistling Pines residents. His name is Henry Oldham."

Tubby tugged at my sleeve. "What happened?" he asked again.

Deputy Harris patted Tubby on the arm and said, "Your friend, Henry, was injured by a bull. He's in pretty bad shape."

"Who are you?" Tubby asked.

"I'm Deputy Harris, from the sheriff's department."

"I don't have a friend named Henry," Tubby replied. "I was here with Tinker."

Harris gave me a questioning look. I responded by explaining that Tinker is Henry's nickname.

"Can we get this show on the road?" Tubby asked. "I need to sit down."

In the pen beside us, a redheaded girl was grooming a red Angus calf the same color as her hair. She was trying to appear disinterested while sneaking furtive looks at the hubbub.

"Excuse, me, could we borrow your chair?" I asked her.

Her name tag said "Megan." With her hair tied in a ponytail and her freckled face she looked no more than 14 years old. She went quickly to the corner and carried a folding canvas camp chair to me. Tubby sat down hard and looked tired.

"Does your father need a drink of water, too?" Megan asked.

"That would be very nice, thank you," I replied, having misplaced my bag of bottled water during the commotion.

Megan hurried to a cooler in the corner of the stall and pulled out a milk jug. She poured water into a Dixie cup, she took from a stack standing on the railing. I had a sinking feeling thinking about the germ content of non-chlorinated well water, stored in a plastic milk jug, poured into a cup that had been sitting in the open pen. Salmonella and E. coli came to mind, but I tempered that with the knowledge that Megan had probably been drinking it for a day and was showing no ill effects. I handed the cup to Tubby, who drank greedily.

"Megan, did you see what happened?" I asked. Deputy Harris moved to the railing to hear her response.

"Umm, I don't know. It all happened kinda fast."

"Do you know the boy who was leading the bull?" Harris asked.

Megan's face flushed and she looked down the aisle to where a good-looking teenaged boy, maybe two years older than Megan, was talking to one of the deputies. She quickly looked at her shoes.

"His name is Tony Benson," she replied. The flush didn't fade.

"He was working with his bull in the pen. Do you know what happened?" I asked.

"He was getting Cosmo ready for the show ring," she replied. "Then Cosmo went kinda nuts and started bucking and kicking."

"Does Cosmo go nuts often?" I asked.

Megan shrugged, looked furtively at a pen across the aisle and said. "I don't think so. The Bensons live a couple miles down the road but I'm not over there much. They raise Angus and which are pretty docile, not like the Charolais that can be mean."

"Did something happen that made Cosmo go nuts?" Harris asked.

Again, Megan flushed. "I think someone shot him?"

"Shot him?" I asked. "I didn't hear a gunshot."

"Not with a gun. He was shot with a binder," she said, making a motion like she was drawing back a rubber-band and then releasing it.

"Someone shot him with a rubber-band and he started kicking?" Harris asked skeptically. Megan nodded in response.

"Where did the rubber-band hit Cosmo," I asked.

Megan was in full red distress now, with the flush creeping up her neck and onto her freckled face. Even the scalp under the part through her hair was red. She leaned across the top rail of the pen and whispered to us, "It hit his...equipment." I looked around and estimated that the bucket serving as her calf-grooming chair put her at eye level with the "equipment" in the neighboring pen.

"Did you see who shot Cosmo?" I asked, trying to lead the conversation into territory that might be more comfortable for Megan.

"I'm not sure. I was kinda looking at Cosmo. I just saw the rubber-band falling and Cosmo went gonzo."

Harris thanked her and took her name and phone number while I looked among the mixed straw and bedding that littered the aisle between the pens. In less than a minute, I saw a bit of red peeking through some scattered straw. I carefully pushed the straw aside with my toe, exposing a heavy rubber-band, like the ones used to hold bunches of broccoli together in the grocery store. It was nearly a quarter-inch wide and about four inches in diameter. A rubber-band of that size had quite a bit of stretch, and a fair amount of momentum. If it were fully stretched, I wouldn't want to be hit in the arm with it, not to mention "my equipment."" There was no wonder that Cosmo reacted to the impact.

"Deputy Harris, can you come over here for a minute?" I asked, interrupting his interview of a nearby teenage boy who was in the pen across from Megan.

As Harris approached, I squatted down and pointed to the rubber-band. "Look what I found inside the bull's pen."

Harris considered the rubber-band and then looked at me skeptically. "Do you think this really hit Cosmo?"

"I think Megan was too embarrassed to have made up the story, and this is roughly where Cosmo was standing when he started bucking." I paused and saw that Harris was still skeptical. But I pointed to the scuff marks made by Cosmo's kicking hooves on the rough cement floor. "How much pain would this cause your equipment?" I asked.

"Stand here," Harris said before disappearing into a mass of people. Since the crowd had broken up once the EMT left, there was little for me to do except swat at the thousands of flies that were attracted by the cattle and manure. I tried to visualize where someone could stand to shoot a rubber-band meant to hit Cosmo. Depending on the strength of the shooter, the range of the binder was probably less than ten or fifteen feet, and to get the angle, the shooter had to be standing in an arc of less than thirty degrees in the aisle directly behind the bull's pen. I looked around the floor and saw at least a dozen other red rubber-bands among the straw in the aisle. I quickly surmised that the shooter had been practicing for a while before his shot went between the wood slats and connected with Cosmo's equipment. In less than a minute Harris was back and I pointed out other rubber-bands.

"I think our shooter was practicing for a while before he connected with Cosmo. Considering what happened, he's probably at the top of the Ferris wheel right now."

"The sheriff thinks it's a prank gone awry," Harris said. "We don't have time to hunt down a rubber binder sharpshooter."

I tried to protest, but he waved me off and I went back to tending Tubby, who was fidgeting in his chair. "Is something wrong?" I asked.

"I gotta pee," Tubby replied. "It's those damned water pills."

His efforts to push himself from the canvas chair were foiled by the soft chair arms that sagged as he pushed. I positioned myself at his side and lifted his arm as he pushed with the other. With wobbling legs he stood, staring at the end of the barn, the aisle crowded with fairgoers. The door leading to the restrooms was some fifty feet distant.

"I can't make it that far," he said, with beads of sweat forming on his brow as his breath quickened. "Get me over to the corner of the pen, where the post will hide me."

"I don't think that's a good idea." Ignoring me, Tubby shuffled to the far corner and pulled his fly open. Before I could intervene, urine was splashing on the concrete floor and straw bedding. The combination of the diuretics and prostate problems made this an excruciatingly slow process, and it drew the attention of everyone in the area, including poor Megan, who got a front row view of the show. Again the part in her hair was glowing from embarrassment while she tried to busy herself with her calf.

Tubby zipped up and shuffled back to the chair blissfully unaware of the scene he'd created. He fell, more than sat, in the chair and tried to catch his breath. "Whew, that was close," he said with a wheeze.

Deputy Harris was frowning and shaking his head. Tubby saw his reaction and puckered his face. "Listen, Sonny, just wait until your prostate swells up to the size of a softball."

Deputy Harris sighed, then nodded to the end of the aisle where the sheriff was speaking with the EMT supervisor and said to me, "The sheriff would like to talk to you."

I made sure Tubby was comfortable, then walked across the aisle to the sheriff. "I'm afraid I can't be much help. I was trying to get Tubby moving along when I saw Tinker moving close to the bull..."

The sheriff waved off my comments. "I understand you're responsible for leading the Whistling Pines group around the fair."

"It's our outing for the week. We come here with several groups every year."

"Whistling Pines is that nursing home where the old guy got stabbed last spring, isn't it?"

"Actually, Whistling Pines isn't a nursing home. Our residents live independently and we provide meals and other services we call assisted living."

"Deputy Harris reminded me that you helped Len Rentz solve that murder," the sheriff said, referring to the Two Harbors Police Chief.

"Well, I asked a bunch of questions, but they didn't seem to go anywhere." I didn't know where the conversation was going, but I had a sinking feeling that I was going to get roped into something.

"Len also told me that when your crazy old neighbor was shooting at rabbits in her back yard you ran toward the shots. Most people either run away or their legs turn to Jell-O."

"There really wasn't much chance that she was going to hit anything. Well, not anything that she was aiming for."

"Len Rentz said that you were very professional. You impressed him."

"Thanks," was the only word I could offer.

"I heard you were thinking about a career in criminal justice."

"A long time ago I was thinking about law enforcement, but I decided to be a recreation director."

"Did you pass the POST exam?" he asked, referring to the eligibility test to be a sworn police officer.

"I did, but my life..." I thought back to the rides with Len Rentz when he tried to convince me to pursue a job with the Two Harbors police. My life had taken a different turn since then. "That was over five years ago; it's only valid for one year," I reminded him.

The sheriff appraised me like the cattle in the judging ring. I wasn't as buff as I'd been in Iraq, but I was still six feet tall and carried about 190 pounds without any paunch. "We're down a deputy and you have the military bearing that makes a deputy effective. Why don't you stop by the courthouse and fill out an application?"

"I appreciate your offer, but like I said, I like the contribution I make at Whistling Pines."

"Do you make a living?" the sheriff asked. "I could probably double your salary."

I'll never get to a middle-class existence but I get by on my salary. I tried to play my trump card. "No one shoots at me. I had enough of that in Iraq."

"No one's ever shot at me," the sheriff replied, "and I've never fired my weapon anywhere but the range. I'd guess that's true for nearly all my deputies."

I put my hands up. "Thanks, but I'm really not interested."

Deputy Harris joined us, a curious smile spreading across his face. He whispered something in the sheriff's ear that had both of them smiling. "You seem uncomfortable with us categorizing the bull incident as a prank and think that it deserves more investigation. I have an option. Raise your right hand. I hereby deputize you as a reserve deputy."

"What does that mean?" I asked as I lowered my hand.

"I authorize you to undertake the investigation of the bull incident. Stop by the sheriff's office and pick up a badge."

Before I could argue further he winked at deputy Harris, turned, and walked away.

Chapter 2

Jenny Chapman, the Whistling Pines nursing director and my girlfriend, was at the far side of the fairgrounds when she'd heard the ambulance siren. Someone told her that one of the residents had been injured in the cattle barn and she came looking for me.

"What happened?" she asked. The heat and humidity left her blonde hair wilted and her face was red and sweaty from her quick walk across the fairgrounds.

I described the bull pen incident to her and explained my theory about the rubber-band. I then told her about the sheriff's reluctance to investigate the incident and my deputization.

"What does that mean?" Jenny asked.

"Since I was persistent about the need for an investigation of the incident, the sheriff appointed me a reserve deputy and assigned me to conduct the investigation."

Jenny grabbed my arm and propelled me down the aisle. Outside the barn, she looked into my eyes. "How bad is Tinker?"

"I think he's badly injured. He was unconscious and they had oxygen on him when they wheeled him to the ambulance. I think he has a punctured lung."

Jenny fumbled for her cell phone and I asked who she was calling.

"The hospital," she said. "I'm going to see if Tinker's there yet, and how he's doing."

"They won't talk to you. There are Federal privacy rules."

"I'm the nursing director; they'll talk to me."

I'd completely abandoned Tubby when Jenny arrived, and suddenly I heard his voice behind me. "I've got to pee again. Do you want me to pee on a post again?"

Hearing that, Jenny spun around. Luckily, someone at the hospital answered Jenny's call before I could get her glare, but she cocked her head and gave me that pleading look that said, "Tell me you didn't really let him pee on a post."

I spotted a sign for the restrooms over a green cement block building outside the barn and I directed Tubby that way. I didn't see a line, so I hoped he'd be able to make it without an accidental release.

"I don't think I can make it," he said, looking at the distant sign. "Let's find a post."

"You can make it. We're only a few feet away. Hang on." I hadn't meant my comment literally, but there I was, escorting Tubby toward the restrooms. He had one hand pulling his oxygen tank and the other clutching his crotch like a kindergartner.

Jenny was waiting at the restroom door when we exited. Tubby was dabbing at a dark spot on his khaki pants with a paper towel. He looked up at Jenny and without embarrassment said, "I had to let go to pull my zipper down."

"That's more than she needed to know," I said to Tubby.

Jenny patted him on the arm. "That's OK. We'll put your pants in the wash when we get home." She was always calm and collected, and always had the right words for the residents.

Jenny directed Tubby toward the parking lot and then held me back as he toddled toward the van. It was an effort on his part, considering that Tubby only made about eight inches of progress with each step as he gasped for oxygen.

"Tinker isn't doing well. You were right, he has a few broken ribs and a punctured lung. They've got him in the ICU but his vital signs haven't stabilized."

I checked my watch and realized that we'd asked the chaperones to deliver their charges to the van about five minutes ago. If history repeated itself, the first would've been waiting for half an hour, and a few would arrive about twenty minutes late, mostly due to the chaperone's failure to estimate how slow a senior citizen walked in August heat.

As we neared the van I could hear Wendy Plauda's distinctive laugh. She had an infectious sense of humor and the residents loved her. I found her both helpful and sometimes infuriating. She knew my hot buttons and she loved to push them. She was rarely around when I needed her, and was always underfoot when I needed her to be somewhere else.

Wendy had rounded up half of the residents and was standing at the van's door, joking with them. It appeared that she'd acquired a stuffed pink elephant in the carnival midway, and was doing a great job of getting everyone involved in a World War II trivia game while they waited for the rest of us to arrive. It was a great theme, since most of the residents couldn't remember this morning, but had vivid memories of many things prior to 1950.

I made a quick count of residents and chaperones and came up only three short. I saw the final threesome making their way down the road, carefully avoiding spilled sodas, chewing gum, and potholes in the gravel driveway. A fall causing a broken hip would really put a capstone on an already hot, miserable day.

Chapter 3

The news about Tinker rippled through the group quickly and took the merriment out of the day. The van ride was subdued. Even Wendy wasn't talking. Jenny contacted the ICU again and learned that Tinker was stabilized and soon a Life Flight helicopter would transport him to Duluth. Elizabeth, Lizzy, Patrone's daughter, one of our stressed-out volunteer chaperones, offered to drive Jenny to Miller-Dwan hospital in Duluth. Because her vigilant daughter was along, Lizzy had been especially careful with her scooter and had only run over a dozen or so toes as she wheeled around the fairgrounds. During last year's trip to the July 4th parade she'd lost control of her scooter and sped through the Moose Lake High School marching band, causing a fair amount of panic.

I promised to retrieve Jenny from Duluth after I'd delivered the senior citizens safely to their rooms.

It was early evening when I got to Duluth. The sun had retreated to the top of the copper-domed church on Skyline Drive when I pulled into the hospital parking ramp. I hoped to pry Jenny loose from the hospital early enough so we could make the forty-minute drive home before the lingering twilight faded and the deer came out to graze in the roadside ditches. I found Jenny at the ICU nurse's station, chatting with the staff.

"Are you ready for a ride home?" I asked.

"Aren't you even going to ask about Tinker?" she asked.

"Sure, how's Tinker, and are you ready to go home?"

"You know that I won't leave until Tinker is stable."

I hugged her and got a feeble hug in return. "Jen, I've been up for nearly eighteen hours and I have only eaten a corn dog all day. The sun is setting and the deer are being chased out of the woods by the horse flies, so they'll be all over the highway once it's twilight. I know you're worried about Tinker, but it's time to worry about you and me right now."

Her hug deepened. "It's just that..." She hesitated. "I just feel like we've let him down."

"I feel like a day-care mom when one of her kids runs into the street," I said. "I shouldn't have let him get hurt, but now he's in the ICU and he's getting the best care possible."

Jenny released her hug and walked to the nurse's station. After a short conversation with the charge nurse she came back and said, "Let's go. Tinker's son will be here shortly and I gave them my cell phone number in case his situation changes."

We walked hand-in-hand to the parking ramp. After exiting Superior Street, driving toward the east end of Duluth that always felt like it was north of downtown, I found the McDonald's at 21st Avenue and pulled into the drive-through. I could tell by Jenny's sigh that Mickey D's wasn't her first choice.

"What would you like?" I asked as I pulled up to the menu board.

"Something that might prevent scurvy," she replied. "Get me a chicken salad with vinaigrette dressing. You might want something that would balance your corn dog, something that has a gram or two of fiber, and maybe even a vitamin."

I ordered Jenny a salad, as directed, then ordered a Big Mac combo, super-sized, with extra lettuce and a Coke. The chill coming from the passenger's seat was palpable, so I said to Jenny, "I got extra lettuce, and I need the caffeine in the Coke to stay awake until we get to Two Harbors."

"Iceberg lettuce really doesn't have any fiber or vitamin content," Jenny said quietly as I waited at the stoplight on 25th, watching a dozen semis turn onto London Road on their way to Canada and points north or east.

"At this point, I'm only interested in getting enough calories and caffeine into my system to make it home safely. I'll do broccoli penance tomorrow and say three Hail Marys."

"You're not Catholic."

"You don't have to be Catholic to do penance."

"Protestants don't do Hail Marys."

We drove silently past the mansions that lined highway 61 and soon we were crossing the Lester River, the easternmost limit of Duluth, as the last sliver of sun peeked through the treetops.

Jenny finally started talking again. "I talked to Mom. Jeremy has a pile of homework and he was less than enthused about giving it his all. I talked to him, but I'm getting the start of the pre-teen sullen attitude from him."

Jeremy is Jenny's son from a former relationship with a handsome Norwegian pilot who flew off before he knew Jenny was pregnant and before Jenny knew he had a family in Norway. Jenny lives with her parents. Her mother, Barbara, works hard to be a June Cleaver role model, and often fills in as back-up mom when work draws Jenny away from her son. I've rarely seen Jenny's mother in anything but a neatly pressed blouse and pleated slacks. Her face is unwrinkled by age or worry. Barbara politely tolerates my relationship with Jenny, but deep down I think she hopes

Jenny will marry a doctor, lawyer, dentist, engineer, or at least someone with a "real" job. She isn't excited about her daughter spending time with "the recreation guy from the nursing home." My one redeeming quality is that Jeremy likes and respects me. I'm also willing and able to help Jeremy with his math homework. The family finds the *new math* too challenging.

I drove through the lingering summer twilight with one hand while biting off pieces of the hamburger, dribbling the special sauce down the front of my shirt. Jenny picked at her salad while occasionally dipping fries into a puddle of ketchup and stuffing a half dozen at a time into my mouth. By the time we got to Two Harbors the last twilight had faded from the sky and Jenny was curled up with her head against the car window, gently sleeping.

Chapter 4

Friday

Friday morning brought fog and the promise of more heat. The weatherman said that the warm, moist air washing north from the Gulf of Mexico was stuck over all of Minnesota. The only hope of a break was a weak cold front that was pushing southeast from Manitoba. The thermometer said it was already 75 degrees when I passed it at 6:30AM, on my walk into Whistling Pines. It was going to be another hot one, at least by North Shore standards.

Having been at the fair all Thursday put my work life in disarray. The usual piles on my desk were covered with message slips and Post-It notes. I brushed them aside and turned on the computer, briefly flipping through the notes while the computer booted up. Nancy, the new Whistling Pines Director, had left a note on top of the pile. In capital letters she'd written, "DON'T FORGET! YOU'RE TAKING THREE RESIDENTS TO THE DOCTOR THIS MORNING!"

Much to everyone's surprise, Kathy, the previous director, had announced her retirement May 1st and on June

1st Nancy Helmbrecht was introduced as the new director. While Kathy had been buttoned down with a smile that almost always looked forced, Nancy had a genuine smile and homey warmth. Though always professional looking, Nancy preferred a business casual wardrobe to Kathy's wool suits. Her two decades of business experience had quickly translated into expectations that made Whistling Pines move along more like a well-oiled machine than our previous work model of crisis management. Nancy let everyone know her smile was genuine and she praised good work, but her expectations were high and she wasn't reluctant to quietly remind you when you hadn't met them.

I had forgotten I was driving three women to the medical clinic, and I would've happily gone ahead with my normal Friday morning duties, including preparations for another trip to the fair, without the reminder.

Seeing no pressing e-mails, I grabbed my chipped yellow happy-face coffee mug and walked to the cafeteria to get a jolt of caffeine.

Barbie Burk was the new dining room coordinator. She replaced Florie, who had inherited a large sum of money when her father, Axel Olson, was murdered. Barbie made sure the table linens were starched, the tables were set with fresh silverware, and each table was adorned with a fresh flower or small floral arrangement. Though slender, that's where Barbie's resemblance to the toy doll ended. Our Barbie had jet black hair and a wardrobe that consisted of tank tops, which she wore under denim overalls with suspenders. She was artistic and every place setting and every vase was carefully set or arranged in a way that appealed to the eye. I'd never noticed anything wrong with Florie's decorations, but Barbie somehow made them look better.

Wendy was already at a table, twirling a pencil and drinking Mountain Dew while she contemplated the crossword puzzle in the *Duluth News Tribune.* She'd turned back the white tablecloth, and pushed the bud vase to the far corner of the table. Wendy is addicted to crossword puzzles. Because of the irregular and vague nature of her responsibilities as assistant director, she was often able to spend hours grinding through the crossword puzzles. Whenever she got stuck, she'd track or flag me down.

"Hi, Wen," I said as I breezed past.

"I need a seven-letter word for pathway and the second letter is an 'O.'"

"Why don't you give up on the *New York Times* puzzle after Tuesday? They get harder each day and you get more frustrated each day."

"I get a great sense of satisfaction from the harder ones."

"But you have to cheat to finish them."

"Peter, it's not cheating to ask a friend for a hint. Come on, what's my word for pathway?"

"Try conduit," I suggested.

She wrote the letters down and then tapped the pencil. After a few seconds, she was busily penciling in other words.

"So, was I right?"

She made a "go away" gesture with her left hand while she wrote with her right.

Breakfast odors emanated from the kitchen, accompanied by Pink Floyd blaring out of a boombox. I stuck my head in the door to check out the menu. Miriam Millam was pouring a couple pounds of chopped carrots into boiling broth. Miriam was funny and philosophical. Now married to her third husband, she helped run a dairy farm while holding down a full-time job cooking at Whistling Pines. She was a sturdy woman whose brown hair was usually in a short, easy-to-manage cut.

Angie Lafond was using a trowel to spread chocolate frosting on a huge pan of brownies. I dipped my finger into the chocolate frosting residue left in a bowl Angie had set aside. Angie was young and spirited, with dyed black hair tied in a hairnet, a pierced eyebrow and a couple of visible tattoos. There were rumors about other tattoos, but it wasn't something that I was going to pursue. Angie didn't have a lot to say, but when she did speak up it was because she had something important to offer.

"Peter! Angie yelled. "Get out of here unless you put on a hairnet! The health inspector was here and I don't want to get written up because you were in here bareheaded licking frosting bowls."

I quickly retreated to the dining room, and found Miriam right behind me. "I heard Tinker got injured by a horse. How's he doing?"

"Well, the rumor mill is churning and turning, and they have already twisted the facts. A bull injured Tinker and he's in the hospital. I honestly don't know how he's doing. They flew him to Duluth and he's in the Intensive Care Unit there."

Miriam frowned. "Are you sure he was injured by a bull? Lots of people get kicked by horses, but not many people are injured by farm bulls."

"I saw it. The bull bucked up and then the gate flew open. It was like a scene from a rodeo."

"Well, those rodeo bulls don't just kick for the fun of it. They've got a harness that makes them kick and buck."

"Someone shot a rubber-band at this one and hit him in...his equipment. That's why he bucked."

Miriam's eyes crinkled and the corners of her mouth turned up as she suppressed a laugh. "His equipment, Peter? We're all big people here. It's okay to say he got hit in the testicles."

Wendy snorted and shook her head. I could feel the heat rising from my neck and migrating to my face. It was the curse of my Scandinavian relatives, who gave me a light complexion and an aversion to talking about body parts.

"Tinker's got a punctured lung and broken ribs," I said, seizing the chance to change the topic. "He was struck by a gate that flew open and he was unconscious when I got there.

"I was chasing him when it happened. Tubby Johnson was lagging behind and Tinker got away from me," I said.

Miriam put her hand on my arm. "It's okay, Peter. Tinker isn't suffering from dementia. He has free will. He can walk ahead of you and it's not your fault if he gets himself into trouble. Tinker was a farmer and he knows the risks of walking through a barn."

Somehow, Miriam worked her philosophical magic and I felt better, like a weight had been lifted. "Thanks."

When I turned, Wendy was gone and the tablecloth was back in place. I briefly wondered if she'd been able to wrap up the crossword with my one hint but the breakfast rush was underway.

Hulda Packer, the source of all misinformation, grabbed me. "I heard Tinker got kicked by a kangaroo at the fair."

"Tinker was bumped by a gate in the cattle barn," I replied.

"Well then, who did the kangaroo kick?"

"I doubt anyone in Lake County has ever been kicked by a kangaroo," I said.

"Are you driving me to the doctor today for my MRE?" Hulda asked. In addition to twisting facts, she had been a teacher with an immense vocabulary that she now often twisted.

"Hulda, an MRE is an army meal. Don't you mean that you're going to have an MRI?"

"No, I'm pretty sure that it's a Muscle Rescue Exam. That would be an MRE."

I was about to correct her and then decided I could better use my time elsewhere. "OK, Hulda, the van is leaving at 8:00."

"8:00! That's hardly enough time to get there and find a magazine. My appointment is at 9:00. What if there's traffic! Better to be an hour early than a minute late, that's what my father taught me."

"We're only a few blocks from the clinic, and there is no traffic. 8:00 is early enough."

"Well, if we're late, it's on your shoulders," she said as she turned and headed for her usual table and her usual breakfast of raisin bran cereal and stewed prunes. As edgy as Hulda generally was, you didn't want to be around her if she hadn't eaten her prunes.

Bessy Linden was right behind Hulda, resplendent in her freshly permed silver hair. It was curled high on her head in an attempt to make her look taller than her actual five-foot stature. "Peter," she said quietly, "I too am going to the clinic for a mammy-o-gram. I hope you can go in and talk to the billing office for me. You know they always try to charge me full price, but they took one boob off when I had the cancer so I should only have to pay half price."

For emphasis, she hefted her left breast and said, "See, this one is a fake boob and it's much lighter than the other one. Just feel it."

I quickly put my hands behind my back. "Bessy, if you've got billing problems, you should talk to Wendy." Wendy, as the director's assistant, handles a broad variety of administrative issues including insurance coverage.

Bessy let her prosthetic boob fall to its normal position and shook her head. "Wendy's way too busy to deal with my insurance problems. She's got her puzzle going, and I hate to interrupt her with something that's a bother, like insurance."

"Trust me. Wendy will be happy to put aside her puzzle to help you with your insurance. She likes helping people with insurance more than anything else."

I escaped from the dining room, only to run headlong into Len Rentz, the Two Harbors police chief. Len bore a strong resemblance to Barney Fife, but was actually a great cop and also my mentor when I was considering a law enforcement career. He was a slender man, and constantly tugged at his service belt to keep it above his non-existent hips. He'd gone back to pipe smoking and a slight odor of pipe tobacco followed him everywhere.

"Whoa, Peter," he said, bracing himself for impact with me.

"Len!" I pulled up short of actually running into him, but stopped well within my Scandinavian comfort zone of about three feet – two feet for relatives. "What brings you out here?"

"I heard that you're the newest Lake County deputy."

"I..."

"You couldn't say no?"

I shrugged. "The sheriff caught me off guard. It would've been inconvenient to say no."

"What are they paying you?"

"The same as you paid – nothing. I think it's important to find out what set off the bull. Tinker Oldham was seriously injured and the sheriff thinks it was just a prank and not worth his time."

"You know it's an election year?" Len asked.

"So?"

"So, if you're deputized and you solve a crime, the sheriff's office gets credit."

"That is so lame," I replied. "What difference does it make who solves a crime?"

"Peter, you are so naïve. If the sheriff isn't solving cases, he can't convince the voters he's tough on crime. That's a big deal to the voters." Len hesitated, then added, "If you're going into law enforcement I'd prefer you join the Two Harbors police force."

"Let me be perfectly clear, I have NO plans to go into law enforcement."

"But you just agreed to be a deputy, right?" Len asked.

"I guess," I replied.

"Do you think there's any link to the people here?"

"I doubt it. Somebody shot a rubber-band at the bull and he erupted. Tinker was in the wrong place at the wrong time. It was probably a kid pulling a prank. Even so, I feel like the prankster should be found and punished."

Len pulled a pipe and a pouch of Honey Cavendish tobacco from his pocket and went through the ritual of loading the pipe. I could almost see the gears turning in his mind as he searched for the right words. After loading the pipe and putting the tobacco pouch back in his pocket, he starting patting his pockets in search of a lighter.

"You can't smoke in here," I reminded him.

"I know. It's part of the rhythm." He clenched the pipe stem between his teeth and sucked on it as if it were lit. "I talked to the sheriff, and he said pretty much the same things you said. He's discounted it as teenagers playing around and causing the ruckus, which is why he didn't assign any of his deputies to investigate."

"Len, I assume that you're here because you don't agree with the sheriff."

"I can't say that I agree or disagree. I know that if you only look one direction, you never see things in the other direction."

"So, why doesn't the sheriff assign a deputy to investigate?"

Len sucked on the pipe and then took a metal tool from his pocket and tamped the tobacco. "Don't sell the sheriff short. His people are busy, but he knows there's an outside chance someone was targeting Tinker or one of the other people who were close to the bull. He also knows you're concerned, so you're his best chance of having someone with investigative skills and who cares about finding the culprit."

"Len, I chose this profession over law enforcement for a reason. Why don't you guys leave me in peace?"

Len smiled. "Neither of us believes that," he said.

"What do you mean, neither of us, you and the sheriff?"

Len smiled as he pointed at himself, and then at me. "Us," he said, and he turned to leave. He hesitated and turned back. "By the way, you should change your screensaver."

"I have floating rectangles as my screensaver." As soon as the words were out of my mouth I got a terrible sinking feeling and ran for my office.

There, scrolling across my computer monitor, was a slideshow of huge bulls, positioned in a way to feature their "equipment." First was the Black Angus, followed quickly by a gigantic Polled Hereford. A breed with horns as wide as Texas slid across the screen as I got into my chair and hit the "escape" button. Nothing happened. I tried to enter my password, only to have it rejected as a Belted Swiss bull, black with a wide white band around his middle scrolled onto the screen. I yelled for Wendy, who's been known to embarrass me by changing my screensaver and other computer settings. A scruffy, brown bull that looked like a Musk Ox, scrolled into view as I was reaching for the electrical plug.

"What?" Wendy asked from my doorway.

"Turn off the bulls."

"Don't you think they're kind of cute?" she asked as she pushed me out of the desk chair and took over the keyboard. A Limousin bull with a long pale body scrolled into view as she punched keys. Suddenly, we were at the home page of a site with the tag line Get Your Big Bull Here! In the corner was an ad for t-shirts emblazoned with the logo, "Nice Bullshirt."

"Are you trying to get me fired?" I asked as I pointed to the door.

"Not really," she said, still sitting in my chair. "I heard that you were playing cop again and the bull theme seemed fitting."

Her face suddenly lit up and she spun around in the chair. "Before I found the big bull site, I found this site. The screen was suddenly filled with the anatomy of a well-endowed man, shown only from navel to knees.

I slammed the door and braced myself against anyone trying to enter. "Wendy, get that off my computer and erase any evidence that it's ever been there!"

"Geez, don't have a calf." Her hands flew over the keyboard and the image disappeared, revealing my usual computer desktop. Another few keystrokes took her to a screen of options and within seconds a clock was ticking as the computer told us it was deleting history.

"There," she said, pushing herself up from my chair. "All back to boring usual."

"Why do you do this to me?" I asked as I resumed the chair and clicked on the icon for accessing our in-house e-mail program.

"I don't know. I suppose it's because you're so easy to embarrass. Or, it might be because you're such a computer novice that you can't stop me from doing whatever I want."

"I put a password on my screensaver to keep people out," I protested.

"Yeah, right, like "JENNY" wouldn't come to mind as your first password choice. You should at least make it challenging for me."

"Wendy, I don't want to challenge you. I want you to stay off my computer."

"My desk is right outside the director's office. How am I supposed to access my personal e-mail if I don't use your computer?"

"Torture someone else for a while, or use the computer in the library, like the residents and housekeeping people do."

Wendy developed a broad, mischievous smile. "What fun would that be?" she asked as she disappeared out the door.

I was deep in my e-mail when a knock on my door brought me out of computer stupor. Nancy, the director, was standing there. I raced through possible scenarios of screw-ups, but couldn't come up with anything except that someone had walked into my office and seen the scrolling bulls.

"I had Wendy change my screensaver back to the floating rectangles," I offered, half as apology.

"That's nice. Did she do that before the people started lining up for their ride to the doctor?"

I pulled the van keys out of my desk drawer and hopped out of my chair. "I'm on it," I said, waiting for her to step aside so I could run to the door and my waiting patients.

"Based on what I've heard, you should probably lock your computer so the bulls don't return," she said as I put the keys in my pocket. She was smiling, so I figured she'd been in on the joke with Wendy or at least knew it wasn't my choice of screensaver.

As I stood, I entered a few keystrokes to lock the computer and return it to the usual screensaver. When I turned, Nancy was still standing in the door.

"I heard that the sheriff asked you to apply to be a deputy. Does that mean that you're leaving?"

"No. I like it here."

"Exactly what happened at the fair yesterday?" she asked.

"A bull went nuts when Tinker was walking past and he got injured."

"Does the sheriff think a crime is involved?"

"We talked to a girl who saw the bull get hit with a rubber-band that appears to be the cause of his episode."

"It hardly seems likely that a rubber-band would cause a bull to rampage," Nancy observed.

"It was a really strong rubber-band and it hit him in a painful spot."

"Like the eye?"

"Um, further back. The witness said that he was hit in his equipment." I could feel the red creeping up my neck.

"Hit his equipment?" Nancy asked.

"Testicles," I replied, feeling the red reach my temples. Somehow explaining this to Nancy was like having the "sex talk" with my mother.

"Ouch. Hence the bull parade on the computer?"

"I'd better run so no one misses an appointment," I said as I pushed past her.

Chapter 5

Sitting in the clinic waiting room afforded me plenty of time to mull over the events in the cattle barn. I could now visualize the crowd of people shuffling ahead of me and Tinker sliding along the edge of the cattle stalls. I was so focused on Tinker and Tubby that I had no recollection of any of the other faces; it was just a sea of bodies surging ahead of me. I'd forgotten, but I now remembered hearing the bull roar, probably in pain, a fraction of a second before I saw Tinker crushed by the gate. People scattered as the bull bucked. Many people escaped down the aisle as the bull's owner struggled to gain control. I was moving toward Tinker, fighting the flow of people as they fled the scene of the raging bull. The bull settled down and the young handler moved him away from the open gate where Tinker lay on the ground. After the EMT took over, I ran back to Tubby to make sure he was safe, and then the deputies arrived. There was nothing useful in my memory.

The mammogram went quickly, but Bessy again grumbled about the cost of having only one breast examined, while being charged for two. Bea Robbins, who was a little less lucid than some of our residents, was quite pleased by her doctor visit. She'd had a few skin abnormalities removed for biopsy, but remembered nothing but the delightful doctor and the glass of orange juice they'd given her – no pain and no complaints.

I left the van's air conditioner running when I went into the hospital to retrieve Hulda Packer from her MRI or MRE, depending on who you believed. Hulda was sitting in the lobby when I arrived. She pushed herself out of the chair and met me halfway across the lobby.

"It's about time," Hulda said as she passed me. "I was done with the doctor hours ago."

I helped Hulda up the three steps into the van and then closed the doors. In the short trip from the air-conditioned van to the air-conditioned lobby, and back again, I'd developed sweat stains on my dark blue shirt. I noticed that Bessy wasn't as tall as she'd been earlier in the morning; the humidity was taking its toll on her new perm.

As the van pulled onto the street, Hulda stepped across the aisle and slid into the seat behind me and said, "You know that Tinker Oldham wasn't much of a farmer."

"Was his farm near Two Harbors?"

"No," Hulda replied. "He farmed down in the swamp country by Mahtowa. He's here because his kids live north of Duluth."

"You said he wasn't much of a farmer. What do you mean?"

"He didn't really farm as much as he raised animals. I think he bought a lot of old horses and mules and had a riding farm. He had the most pathetic bunch of sway-backed old nags that I'd ever seen, and he never took care of the fences. Cars hit two of his mules, and the neighbors shot a couple horses when they repeatedly raided their gardens. I assume the poor things were just trying to find food, because he didn't have enough pasture for the number of animals he had, and he never put up enough hay to feed them through the winter."

"It sounds like the humane society or someone would be after him."

"Not in the old days. People minded their own business and we stayed out of the neighbors' business. People beat their wives and others molested children. Tinker neglected his horses. Sometimes a person might meet up with vigilante justice, and sometimes an angry father or jealous husband would exact retribution. It's just the way things were."

"Did Tinker ever get retribution?"

"He went broke, so I guess that's one form of retribution. He sold all his horses to a glue factory or something and took a job in Duluth at the horseshoe factory. Then the horseshoe factory went under and he went to work in the paper mill. Every time he started to get ahead, bad luck hit him again. In the end all he had left was a few tools so he started his fix-it business to supplement the few dollars he got in pension."

"His wife and kids stuck with him?" I asked.

"Sure. There weren't many options in those days. One of his boys joined the army when he turned seventeen and was killed in Viet Nam. His daughter got pregnant and married a hothead who beat her regularly until she shot him. I think she's out of prison now. The youngest son decided to be a farmer and bought a place out in Alden Township. He raises a few cattle, and he does taxidermy on the side. He was the brightest of the bunch, and he seems to be doing OK."

"What happened to Tinker's wife?"

"She had a bout of breast cancer when he was between jobs and didn't have insurance. By the time she went to the doctor it was too late to treat it. They made her comfortable and she died after a couple of months. I suppose some people looked on that as divine justice. I thought it was a tragic end to a life filled with bad choices, starting with her decision to marry Tinker."

"How do you know about all this?" I asked.

Hulda shrugged. "Some I heard from my sister in Mahtowa. The rest I heard from the other folks after his move to Whistling Pines."

I measured her lucidity and wondered how much I should discount her comments based on her jumbled memories.

Chapter 6

I pulled under the Whistling Pines portico, helped the ladies down the steps and guided them through the front door. As I parked the van, I ran Hulda's comments through my mind. Was it possible that someone with a grudge about the treatment of Tinker's horses seized an opportunity to teach him a lesson? What were the odds that someone like that would have a supply of rubber-bands in hand, would be able to take several practice shots without drawing notice, and would have the perfect angle on Cosmo to put him into a rage? Megan had looked at a stall across the aisle when I asked who might've shot the errant binder.

Every angle I looked at made me more convinced that a prankster had taken his shot and Tinker happened to be in the wrong place at the wrong time.

Jenny met me in the lobby and nodded toward the large aviary on the west wall of the atrium. With the lovebirds cooing in the background, Jenny said, "Tinker is out of the coma and talking to the nurses." She was visibly relieved.

"Is his prognosis for recovery good?"

"He's not a kid, so the healing process won't go quickly, but at least he's out of the woods for now. He has several broken ribs, so it pains him to take a deep breath, which of course, counterbalances the doctor's wishes to have him breathe deeply and cough so he doesn't get pneumonia."

"Is pneumonia of concern? Can't they treat him with antibiotics?"

"They're filling him with antibiotics, but if he can't clear his lungs..." Jenny paused to collect herself. "When our seniors fall down and break a hip, it's not the broken hip that kills them, it's the pneumonia that follows."

"I thought you had good news."

"That was good news. It's just that we have to temper it with a little reality."

"So, are we taking a deep breath and hoping for the best? Does that mean that we can take the weekend off and do something fun?"

Jenny smiled and I melted. She could've asked me to drive to San Diego and I would've been gassing up the car. "Remember? Jeremy asked you to take him to the county fair tomorrow," she said.

My less than enthusiastic expression must've leaked through my happy façade because she quickly added, "I know you've already been there, but I was hoping it could be a bonding experience."

I put on my best smile and took her hand in mine. "I'm sorry. It slipped my mind in all the commotion."

Jenny hugged me and whispered, "Thanks for being a good sport. Jeremy's going to an overnight birthday party tomorrow after the fair and my parents want us to have dinner with them."

I was first excited that Jeremy was engaged for the night, hoping that would free Jenny for our own sleepover, then deflated when I heard about the dinner plans. Jenny's parents were stalwart members of the community who intimidated me with their starched-shirt attitude and model-home décor that looked like no one ever sat on the couches.

As usual, Wendy was walking by at the most inopportune time and shook her head. "Why don't you two get a room?"

Jenny winked at her and said, "We will," as she released her hug and walked away.

I walked back to my office and surprised Nancy, who was writing me a note.

"Peter," Nancy said, picking up the note and handing it to me, "I had a call from John Carr, the Two Harbors City Band director. They have a problem."

"What's the problem?" Everyone in Two Harbors knew John Carr. He'd been the director of the Two Harbors City Band since anyone could remember. The band is the longest standing city band in Minnesota with roughly fifty dedicated people ranging from high school musicians to octogenarians. They were most noted for their Thursday evening concerts in the Thomas Owens Park bandshell during the summer, which Jenny and I often attended.

"John broke his heel," Nancy explained. "The band is scheduled to perform at the county fair on Saturday night and he'd like you to fill in as director."

I was dumbfounded, which Nancy mistook for reluctance. "Peter, this would generate a lot of goodwill for Whistling Pines. I'd like you to do this."

"I'm honored to be asked, but Saturday is tomorrow. I'm not sure I'm qualified and there's no time to prepare."

"You'll do very well," she said as she handed me the phone number.

Chapter 7

I dialed the number. A male voice answered, "Hello, this is John."

"Hi, this is Peter, from Whistling Pines. I had a message to call you."

"Peter, how good of you to call. I'm sure Nancy already told you about my dilemma. Is there any chance that you can direct the City Band tomorrow night?"

"Mister Carr, I'm really honored to be asked, but I'm not sure I'm qualified."

He laughed. "I saw you sit in with the Gin Fizzes at Hugo's Bar last spring. You have a great voice and you were the best musician on the stage." He asked, "How many instruments can you play?"

"I'm pretty good on the piano and guitar. I've dabbled with the alto sax, flute, and clarinet, but I wouldn't be comfortable playing any of the woodwinds in public."

Carr laughed and said, "I have a lot of good musicians, but you'll be among the most versatile musicians there. You'll do fine." He paused and added, "Besides, you can't be too good or the band won't want me back again."

I let out a deep sigh and looked at the calendar. "It's already Friday and I've never seen the music. Is there a practice tonight?"

"Most of the band is attending the fair today, so we didn't plan for another practice before the show. I'll have Brian Johnson, one of the tuba players, drop off the music this afternoon so you can look at it. He may be a little pouty because he's the backup director, but since he's one of only two tuba players, he'll have to deal with it."

"Oh great," I thought, "I'll have an unhappy tuba player on top of having no credibility with the band."

"Peter, you've heard the tuba player jokes?" John asked, interrupting my thoughts.

"I'm afraid not. Are there a lot of tuba jokes?"

"For some reason, tuba and trombone players seem to be a little different," John said. "Anyway, there are two tuba players in a car. Who's driving?"

"I don't know."

"The cop."

I had a vision of two men in the back of a police car with their tubas, and let out a groan.

"The band plays at 3:00 tomorrow afternoon and most of the musicians will be there half an hour early. Have fun! They're a good bunch and you'll do well."

"I'll try."

I went to the restroom and when I returned to my office I found Wendy sitting at my desk staring at the computer. At first I was irritated that she'd taken over my computer again, and then I looked at the computer screen and froze.

She turned and looked at me, and then turned back to the computer without comment.

"Wendy, why are there naked women on my computer?"

"Your computer is locked up and they won't go away," she said.

"I can see that," I said, "but why did they show up there at all? When I left, the screensaver was flashing swirling rectangles against a black background that should've been protected by my password."

Wendy gave me a disgusted look and said, "That terribly secure new password, 'Angus'?"

"That's not obvious," I protested. She waved off my protest.

"I was curious," she replied.

"You were curious about naked women?"

"I had another crummy date with a scumbag I met at one of the band gigs," she said, her fingers now flying over the keyboard with no apparent effect on the locked screen.

"And what has a scumbag date got to do with naked women on my computer?"

"I decided that maybe I had a problem with guys. At first I thought that maybe I was being too picky, and that I needed to lower my standards. Then, after the scumbag, I decided that I couldn't let my standards get that low. I figured that maybe I needed to enter a convent, but that seemed a little too drastic, so then I decided that maybe I should try being a lesbian."

I was speechless. I'd worked with Wendy for several years and had seen her performing with The Gin Fizzes. She flirted shamelessly with anything male and seemed hypersexual if anything. She'd flirted with me when I'd started at Whistling Pines but quickly decided that I was too boring to be of interest. Her tastes seemed to run toward guys with a bad boy image.

"I don't think that people make a decision to change their sexual orientation," I said. "I think they discover that they're attracted to either men, or women, and that's just the way they're wired."

She stopped keyboarding to stare at the naked forms on the computer screen and then commented. "You're probably right. These bimbos just aren't lighting my fire like a cute guy with a manly moustache." She spun in the chair and walked to the door.

I sat at the keyboard and tried a number of keystrokes to make the naked ladies disappear. Nothing I keyed had any effect. I moved the mouse and noticed that the cursor was locked in one spot near the behind of a full-figured girl chasing a volleyball.

"Don't bother," Wendy said as she left. "It's locked up. You'll have to do a hard shut down and hope that the screen is gone when the computer restarts." With that, she was gone from the scene of her crime.

I was holding the power switch, waiting for the five second delay before the computer started a hard shut-down when I heard someone entering my office. I prayed it wasn't Nancy, who would probably fire me on the spot if she caught me with porn on my computer screen.

"Peter, could you..." The question froze a second before the computer screen went blank. "What are you looking at?" Jenny asked.

"Wendy was looking at nude women to see if she is a lesbian," I quickly explained.

"What? No."

"Really," I said as the computer screen went black. "Wendy had another bad date and decided that maybe she was really into women and that was why she was having so many problems dating guys."

"So, her solution was to pull up images of nude women on your computer?"

"Scout's honor," I said holding up my right hand in the three-fingered Boy Scout oath. "You can ask her."

Jenny wasn't pleased, but left, having forgotten whatever it was that had brought her to my doorway, and before I could tell her about my gig as the substitute City Band director.

To my great relief, the computer prompted me for my password and opened to my usual desktop. I put it into sleep mode, and briefly wondered if I could find the key to lock my office. I quickly dismissed the idea. Even if I could find a key buried somewhere in a desk drawer, Wendy has a master key that can open any of the few locked doors in the whole of Whispering Pines. I picked up the September activities schedule and went to the little cluster of offices near the entrance to run copies. Nancy was on the phone, so I started the copies and stuck my head in the nursing office where Jenny was studying a medical file in a red three-ring binder.

"You'll never guess who's filling in as the guest director for the Two Harbors City Band tomorrow night," I said.

She looked up and I could see how tired she was. "Are they playing at the bandshell?"

"They're playing at the fairgrounds and John Carr has a broken heel." The idea of directing the band was starting to grow on me.

"I don't think we have time to stay around to hear the concert," she said. "We're taking Jeremy to the fair and then we're having dinner with my parents."

Before I could respond, Wendy pushed past me and sat in the extra chair. "It's so unfair that they'd ask Peter to be the fill-in director and not me."

"What?" Jenny asked.

"John Carr asked Peter to be the fill-in director for the City Band tomorrow night. Peter's not even from Two Harbors. How can he be the director of the City Band?"

"How do you know that?" I asked. "I only talked to him twenty minutes ago."

Wendy gave me a sly grin, but didn't answer. She set a crossword puzzle on the desk and plucked a pen from a cup emblazoned with the Paxil logo.

"That's great, Peter," Jenny replied with an edge to her voice. "I'll have to call my mother and tell her that we'll have to reschedule our dinner with them."

My heart deflated like someone stepping on a ketchup package. "Dang it." My reply lacked sincerity.

"You have to direct the band," Wendy said. "It's a big honor."

"I'm sure your mother will understand," I said, trying to recover some dignity. "They love going with us to the summer concerts. You should invite them to the fair concert and we can go out to eat afterward."

"Why don't you call your mother, too," Jenny suggested. "I'm sure that she'd come up from Duluth to watch her son's directing debut."

The slight rebound that I'd got from suggesting that Jenny's parents come to the band concert was quickly offset by the thought of my mother driving from Duluth to watch the Two Harbors City Band at the county fair. Mother and I have a good relationship as long as we limit our contact to a Sunday evening call that recaps her week, after which I say, "I love you" before hanging up.

My mother is a very artistic person who lives her life through her charitable activities. She serves meals at the teen rehab facility three days a week. She is a docent at the Duluth railroad museum. She is a volunteer reader at the library's "children's hour," and she personally has adopted two miles of highway 210 near Carlton, where she rallies her friends as she leads the caravan of helpers to pick up trash three times a year. Every winter, the Lester Park Community Theatre stages three plays and mother always has a role in each of them, her position cemented by her ability to emote on stage and her generous contributions. She's rarely found time for me, her only child, except for our Sunday evening call. The conversations are always one-sided and have only one topic: Mother.

My father had been a successful criminal lawyer in Duluth, which left my mother free of the burdens of needing a second income, managing a household budget, paying bills, or even knowing how much money they had or where the money was located. When my father was killed in an accident on I-35 while driving to a trial in Carlton County, his life insurance went into a trust, along with the cash from his partners buying out his share of the law practice. The trust provides mother a handsome monthly check which she shares freely. She embodies the stereotype of the guilty rich Democratic Party supporter.

The money allows her to do all the philanthropic things she wants, without the worry of paying for "things." The major source of friction between us is my matching trust account. I choose not to draw on it, preferring to live on my Whistling Pines income, rather than my father's legacy. Our second source of friction is that I haven't produced an heir to Father's fortune. That's led to a third source of friction, which is Jenny, who already has a son. "You can do better than marrying a woman with baggage," Mother repeatedly tells me.

"My parents haven't met your mother. This may be our chance," Jenny was saying.

Jenny's mother is perfect. Barbara has sculpted beauty and poise, neither of which ever cracks or wrinkles. Her clothes are always freshly pressed, her makeup tasteful, her jewelry understated, limited to tiny diamond stud earrings and a wedding band. Jenny's father is a successful insurance broker. Howard drives a Cadillac, plays golf, drinks martinis, and never swears. He's voted a straight Republican ticket in every election since turning 21.

My mother, Audrey, puts on makeup with a trowel and wears flowing dresses designed to cover her expansive girth. Jewelry is more than an accessory for her, it's her persona.

My father showered mother with jewelry for birthday and Christmas presents. She drapes her neck with mismatched necklaces and she wears dangling earrings and gold bangles that clank against each other when she waves her arms. And she always waves her arms. Her arms flail emphatically through all conversations as if she was on stage. And she talks, ranting about poor funding of the schools, the Nazi tactics of the Republican Party, the unfairness of property taxes, and whatever she's adopted as her latest charity cause. She gives generously and works tirelessly for every Democratic Party candidate who holds elective office in Duluth. After a couple glasses of wine she swears like a drill instructor when she argues politics.

I loathed the thought of her sharing a table with Jenny's quiet, polished, Republican parents who wouldn't say "shit" if they had a mouthful of it.

Jenny was reading my mind, a super power she uses routinely. "They have to meet sometime," she said.

"Can I come along? I like Peter's mother." Wendy had been in several musical productions at the Lester Park Theatre and knew my mother well. Wendy also knew I was uncomfortable with my maternal relationship and loved to poke me when she had the chance.

"I'll give mother a call," I said as my stomach churned.

"Peter," Wendy said as I turned to leave. "Who was the killa in Manila?" she asked, staring at the crossword puzzle.

"Mohammed Ali," I replied.

Wendy looked at the puzzle and frowned. "It's only three letters."

"A-L-I,"

"Perfect!" she said, filling the letters in the squares. She jumped up and pushed past me. "I've got to gas up the van. I'll see you under the portico in fifteen minutes."

"How do you know all the answers?" Jenny asked, having seen me supply a correct answer for every crossword clue that Wendy posed.

"They just come to me."

Jenny looked around and handed me a doctor's order. "Read this."

"What?"

"Just read it," she replied.

I quickly scanned the document and returned it to her. "Hulda Packer is having a minor surgical procedure," I said. "So what?"

"How are they doing the procedure?"

"Laproscopically."

"Spell it for me."

"L-A-P-R-O-S-C-O-P-I-C-A-L-L-Y."

"Where does it say that in the note?"

"It's the eighth word of the fourth sentence in the second paragraph."

Jenny smiled. "You have a photographic memory. That's why I've never seen you read music when you play. You can remember all the notes."

I shrugged.

"How far back can you remember?" she asked.

"I used to be able to remember things back to grade school. I lost a lot in Iraq."

"Lost it because of the physical or mental trauma?" she asked.

"I don't know," I said, flashing back to the inside of the Humvee rolling after being struck by the shock wave from an exploding IED. My helmet protected my head as it banged against the ceiling and both sides before the Humvee came to rest with me lying on the ceiling. I'm sure Marines were yelling for me, the corpsman, but it was several days before my hearing returned. I climbed out and, out of instinct, responded to what I saw as the greatest carnage. I was later told that there were bullets ricocheting off the armored trucks all around me and the Marines were impressed with my selfless attempts to rescue their buddies. In reality, I didn't react to the ricochets because

I couldn't hear a thing. The next day Lieutenant Pittman, a new Annapolis graduate, stopped me after lunch and slapped me on the back. He told me I was either crazy or some damned brave idiot who didn't know enough to keep my head down during a firefight. He thanked me for dragging one Marine out of withering crossfire and behind the Humvee. He said he'd nominated me for the bronze star with a V for valor. I was still half-deaf and too embarrassed to tell him I couldn't hear the gunfire.

Jenny saw me glaze over and quickly moved to pull me back from Iraq. "Are you okay with your mother meeting my folks at the fair?"

After a moment I was able to clear the Iraq memories and answer. "Mother dresses like a gypsy and argues with Republicans. What can go wrong?"

"They'll be together at a wedding someday," Jenny replied.

"I may not pop the question until after mother dies."

"How old is she?"

I did the math in my head. "She's fifty-something."

"She wants a grandchild."

I froze at the reality of Jenny's words. "Probably," I replied.

She pulled me close and whispered in my ear. "We're both in our thirties. Having a child together might not be a sure thing in a few years."

Chapter 8

I grabbed the Friday sign-up list for the van and hurried to the front door where the residents were lining up for the ride. Howard Johnson, the self-appointed "Mayor" of Whistling Pines, was near the front of the line. He was a magnet for the disgruntled and meek residents who, for whatever reason, were unwilling to take their grievances to the management. He was having a hushed discussion with Dottie Preston. Dottie blushed and turned away as I approached.

"Howard, I was surprised to see your name on the list for the van. I thought you'd drive yourself to the fair."

Howard, impeccably dressed in a white golf shirt and khaki pants with a crease that could cut butter, smiled. "The parking at the fair is terrible, and you drop us at the front gate. It's much easier."

I motioned for Howard to follow me to the aviary, a few feet away from the entrance. "What's Dottie's issue?" I asked. I anticipated that she was concerned about Tinker's injuries.

Howard turned his back to the people in line and leaned close to my ear. "Dottie heard that you'd been asked to fill in for the City Band conductor and is a little upset because you're not from Two Harbors." Howard mistook my smile for impertinence. "Did I say something funny?"

"Not at all," I replied. "I only received the call this morning and I think it's funny the news has already hit the Whistling Pines party line."

Howard smiled. "It's not surprising at all. John Carr called me last night to ask if you were really up to the task. I told him that you played a half dozen instruments, had an amazing ear, and a degree in music from the university. I think that your qualifications are better than anyone in the band."

"That's very kind."

Howard patted my shoulder. "Too bad you're not from around here."

Chapter 9

I'd drawn two women, Pixie Kangas and Connie Danielski, as my two seniors for the day and instead of a tour of the livestock barns we shuffled to the 4H building where the art and craft projects were displayed. The projects ran from paintings to photographs to homemade quilts and woodworking. We stopped at each, weighing the quality of the workmanship against the family lineage of the creator.

Pixie was examining a taxidermy mount of a large northern pike. The workmanship was crude, reflecting the age, thirteen, of the artist. The eyes were too large, the white spots were irregular, and the skin, which should've been smooth, was rippled where it had been folded or mishandled. The mouth was open and he'd apparently filled it with plaster of Paris that he'd painted pink.

"Oh dear," Pixie said. "Shelby's grandson did this fish and I can't even tell what type of trout it is."

"I think it's a Northern Pike," I replied. "Look at the teeth."

Connie, who was in need of cataract surgery, stared in the fish's mouth. "It looks like a big mouth bass to me. They're not much for eating, but the boys sure had a good time catching them."

"I think the judges should give him at least a white ribbon," Pixie said. "His father volunteers at the animal shelter and he's such a nice man."

"Don't you think the judges should choose the best workmanship?" I asked.

"Oh, I don't think so," Connie said. "You don't want to give a prize to some stinker just because his work is good, do you?"

I let the question dangle as we made our way through the rest of the steel building. We stopped at the Lutheran Church lunch counter and had coffee and homemade doughnuts. By the time we got on the van I was mentally wasted and physically exhausted.

A man I didn't recognize was sitting on the bench under the Whistling Pines portico wearing a Tyrolean hat and Lederhosen. A nylon briefcase hung from a shoulder strap. He approached me as the last of the oldsters left the van. He offered his hand and introduced himself. "I'm Brian Johnson. John Carr said you'd be expecting me."

I estimated him to be about sixty, with a round face, thinning dark hair, and bushy eyebrows. He was stocky, like many of the tuba players I'd met.

"Ah," I said, shaking his hand. You're Brian the tuba player who is bringing music."

Brian saw my reaction to his outfit and said, "I just came from the fair. My polka band was playing at the fairgrounds."

"Your outfit isn't something I'd expect to see wandering Two Harbors," I said.

He slid the briefcase strap from his shoulder. "Is there somewhere we could sit down to review the music for the concert?"

I directed him to my office and cleared the visitor's chair. "John said you are the assistant director. I hope

I'm not stepping on your toes by taking the baton for this concert."

Brian gave me a sour look as he took the neatly clipped stack of music out of the briefcase and arranged the pages on his lap. Yellow tabs stuck out of the stack. He handed me a single sheet of paper. "Here's the music set we've been practicing for the fair." Handing me a second sheet he said, "And here's the music for the year-end concert at the bandshell."

The first sheet reminded me of the music I'd heard them play when Jenny and I had attended their summer concerts; a variety running from popular songs to big band favorites from the '40s. I looked through the second sheet and noted that all the songs were marches, running from classical composers to the ending with Sousa's "Stars and Stripes Forever."

"How much experience do you have as a conductor?" he asked.

"Well, I have a little conducting experience," I said, reflecting on a Christmas concert I'd arranged in Iraq. "I have a bachelor's degree in instrumental music and a pretty fair ear."

"Humph," he replied. He was unimpressed with my credentials.

"Is there anything special I should know before the concerts?" I took the music and set the pile atop my desk.

"Well," he paused, apparently unprepared for the question. "The band is diverse with high school kids and retirees. The trombone players are mostly goofy. The clarinet players are always mad because the trombone players blow their spit-cocks right behind the clarinet players' chairs."

"How are the trombones goofy?" I asked.

"Well, there's Billy 'Chicken' Paulson. He used to drive down the highway in the wrong lane to make the oncoming cars veer into the ditch. He may be the most normal of the lot."

He paused and then opened up. "I'm not entirely happy with you taking over the band, because I'm the assistant director. But you can't play tuba, and John Carr convinced me that we need a tuba more than we need me as a conductor."

"That's not exactly a vote of confidence."

"It's nothing against you. It's just..."

"I'm not from Two Harbors," I finished.

"Well, there's that. But besides that, you've never played with us. I've heard that you're good, but you've never picked up an instrument with us. I don't even know what you can play. Do you play anything other than guitar?"

"I'm pretty good on guitar, piano, clarinet, and alto sax. I've dabbled with the flute, but skipped most of the brass section when I was learning instruments."

"You're not going to change any of the arrangements, are you?" Brian asked, defensively.

I looked at the pile of music. "Not a chance. I won't have the time even if I wanted to make changes."

Brian smiled. "That's one of the things that can get people's undies in a bunch."

"What else should I avoid?"

"Well, the band's dress code for 'shirt nights' is a white shirt, red tie, and black pants. Show up half an hour early, but don't be surprised if the bassoonist doesn't show up until you're already on the podium. Oh, and don't be surprised if one of the male musicians shows up in a dress."

When I raised my eyebrows, he explained. "Jerald Bowden is in the middle of becoming Jessie. It's no problem when we're wearing our uniforms, but on 'shirt nights' I'm never sure if he'll be in slacks or a skirt. It's not a big deal, it's just a little unsettling not to know. Of course, it's just strange for a six foot guy to show up with his braless "B" cup boobs in a white shirt and ponytail." He paused, and then added, "It's kinda hard not to stare, if you know what I mean."

"I've never met anyone transgender. I'll try not to stare."

The more Brian spoke, the more comfortable he became with me. "Well, just be prepared and know that not everyone is as open minded as you and I are."

I smiled. "You warned me about the trombones, but I've always heard that it was the tuba and bass players who were the troublemakers."

Brian smiled. "Two tuba players are sitting at a bar. Which one is drinking?"

"I don't know."

"It's a trick question. Everyone knows both would be drinking," he replied as he smiled and stood. "I won't cause you any trouble, but look out for the trumpets. They all think that they should be first chair, so John rotates them annually. They may try to make their cases with you."

"Why would they do that? I'm only filling in for a couple weeks."

Brian smiled. "John was a little evasive with you. The season is ending and we only have the county fair concert on Saturday and then the year-end concert in the park bandshell next Thursday. We need you to fill in for both those events and that's plenty of time for people to express their frustrations and distrust."

I was suddenly overwhelmed, given my responsibilities at Whistling Pines, trying to get justice for Tinker, and now filling in as the band director.

Wendy surprised us when she stepped into my crowded office, leaving none of us with adequate personal space. "I heard that you're doing Gilbert and Sullivan for the year-end City Band concert. Peter, I think we should do the Baroness and Rudolph duet."

When she saw my look of surprise she broke into song with her resonant alto voice.

"As o'er our penny roll we sing,
It is not reprehensive
To think what joys our wealth would bring
Were we disposed to do the thing
Upon a scale extensive.
There's rich mock-turtle thick and clear"

She stopped, apparently expecting me to sing the next verse. I was dumbstruck. Brian looked like he was ready to push the crazy woman aside and run.

"I'm afraid I'm not familiar with that song," I said, trying to evade the issue.

Wendy pulled out a sheet of music and lyrics and handed it to me. "You're a really quick study. I'm sure you could master this in a couple of days."

Brian looked at me with panic in his eyes. "The county fair concert is tomorrow night and the last concert is always marches. If we did Gilbert and Sullivan, we'd have to practice and play it earlier in the year."

Wendy gave Brian her best disarming smile and bumped her ample hip into his. "C'mon, it's time for you guys to open up the playlist and have some fun."

Brian, obviously unaccustomed to someone as forward as Wendy, looked like he'd swallowed a peach pit.

"Are you married?" Wendy asked, reveling in his discomfort as his chubby cheeks turned red.

"Um, yes," he replied, lifting his left hand to show his wedding ring.

"Happily married?" she asked, leaning forward and exposing the top of a teddy bear tattoo in her cleavage.

Brian's eyes drifted to the tattoo for a second and then snapped back to Wendy's smiling face. "Yes, happily married."

"It's a pity that all the good ones are taken." With that, she swept out of my office as quickly as she'd appeared.

Brian stared at the open door for a second, and then looked back at me. "Who was that?"

"Wendy is the assistant director and also fills in with the music program. She sings and plays piano. She's also the lead singer for The Gin Fizzes, a local band."

"When we do vocal music my wife is the soloist. She might do you serious harm if she were unexpectedly displaced by your...your tattooed friend."

"Believe me, I have no plans to change anything and I'll be happy to hand the baton back to John when he's well."

"For your sake, I hope that's all you do." With that cryptic comment, Brian was gone.

Chapter 10

Friday evening

I was nearly home when I saw my neighbor, Dolores, waving at me from her front porch. Dolores has no family so she depends on my regular assistance with tasks that are beyond her capabilities.

When I got to the porch with the music under my arm I realized she was wearing only one of her black orthopedic shoes. My gut told me this wasn't a good situation.

"Peter, I'm so pleased you're home," she said, quickly turning her back on me and limping into the house. I reluctantly followed her. She sat in an ancient brocade covered chair and pulled her bare foot onto the matching hassock. She then aimed what appeared to be a cell phone at her foot and held it at arm's length.

"What's up?" I asked.

"I'm trying to get a picture of my toe so I can e-mail it to my doctor." She stabbed something on the face of the cell phone's digital screen with such force that the phone twisted in her fingers. "Damn. I can't get a decent picture"

I looked at Dolores's bare left foot, and saw that her big toe was an ugly shade of black. "What happened to your toe?" I asked.

"The doctor said it's the damned diabetes. I think it's just because I stubbed it on the leg of my dresser," she replied. She reoriented the phone and tried another picture with the same result. "Here, Peter, you take the picture."

I took the cell phone and looked at the unfamiliar screen. "Why do you want a picture of your toe?"

"I told you, I'm going to e-mail it to the doctor. It's getting worse and I can't get the nurse to do anything about it over the phone. I thought that an e-mail directly to the doctor might yield better results than dealing with the help."

Dolores and her husband had been well off and employed a maid and a cook through much of their lives. I shuddered at her characterization of the doctor's triage nurse as "the help".

"Why don't you just get an appointment?" I asked, looking at the screen and locating a button that looked like an electronic version of a shutter release. I framed the toe and gently pushed the button. The screen froze, the phone made an audible click, and we had a perfect picture of Dolores's black toe.

"They charge a co-pay for office visits, but e-mails and phone calls are free," she explained. I handed the phone to her and watched as she moved through screens, then keyed in an e-mail address with her arthritic fingers. I was amazed at her skill in navigating the technology and wondered to myself how many Whistling Pines residents would have the mental acuity and manual dexterity to manage the tiny phone. After a minute she paused and said, "There. Now help me with my hosiery."

I slid her support hose over the discolored toe and stopped discreetly halfway up her calf. "Are you sure you're able to walk around the house with this toe?" I asked.

"Are you joking? I'm going to the fair tomorrow!"

"Isn't the black toe causing you a lot of pain?"

"Oh no," she replied as I carefully slid her heavy orthopedic shoe over the black toe. "It's so much better than when it was purple."

I was tempted to explain that this was an unfortunate series of events that would end in a bad outcome for the toe if it remained black, but she seemed pleased, so I let it pass.

"I heard you are the guest conductor for the City Band concert at the fair. That should be challenging," she said, standing up and teetering for a second.

"How will that be challenging?"

She shuffled to an antique desk and pulled open a drawer. "Well, there are some very interesting people in the band, and some very strong personalities. It's taken an assertive director to keep them all playing on the same page."

She reached into the drawer and withdrew a small case. "I played in the band for thirty years, until I couldn't march in the Heritage Days parade anymore." She shuffled back to me with the tiny case in her hand.

"What instruments do you play?" she asked.

"At Whistling Pines I play piano and guitar most of the time. I've played clarinet, dabbled with some of the other woodwinds and could play most of them with a little practice."

She handed me the box and said, "Give this a try."

Inside the box was a sterling silver piccolo with a tiny inscription in German. I put the box on a table and removed the two pieces, fitting them together gently. "Dolores, this is very valuable. I don't even want to touch it," I said, gently bringing it to my lips and trying to play a few notes. After a few tries, I pinched my lips tight enough to get the piccolo to chirp. The piccolo was much harder than the flute. I played a few notes and then held it to appreciate the fine workmanship.

"Where did you get this," I asked.

"I played piccolo in high school and with the City Band for a few years. I started with a ratty old piccolo that I purchased from a music store in Duluth. It was chipped and scratched, but it played well. I was seeing a young man who was taken with my musical ability. One year for Christmas he gave me this piccolo and promised it would be followed by a diamond ring."

"That was your husband?" I asked.

Tears formed in Dolores' rheumy eyes and she shook a dainty handkerchief from her sleeve. She lifted her glasses and dabbed at her eyes. "Yes," she croaked, unable to say more. She closed her eyes and took several deep breaths. "Please take this. It needs a better home than my dusty drawer."

"I can't accept this. It's too valuable."

"Don't be ridiculous," she said with a smile. "I have no heirs, and who else would appreciate this Gemeinhardt instrument?"

I gently pulled the pieces apart. "Thank you."

"Will you be at the fair tomorrow?" she asked as I put the pieces back into the case.

"I'll be escorting another group from Whistling Pines," I replied. "I'll be there from mid-morning and then Jenny and I are taking her son after that."

"Well then, I'll see you there," she said in an obvious dismissal.

When I got to my front door, I managed to juggle the piccolo and sheet music as I picked up the morning newspaper, but sheets of music flew from my grasp when I tried to twist the doorknob. I slipped the piccolo in my pocket and was gathering the scattered paper when Jenny pulled in the driveway. She helped me retrieve the music and opened the door. We set the music on the kitchen table for later sorting.

I pulled her close and kissed her.

"Mmm. Are you happy to see me, or do you have a banana in your pocket," she said in her best attempt at a Mae West impersonation as she pressed her hips against me.

"Actually, it's a piccolo."

She pushed me back and cocked her head. "Piccolo?" she asked.

I reached in my front pants pocket and took out the tiny case. "Dolores gave it to me when I took a picture of her toe."

"Back up. Why did you take a picture of her toe? Why did she give you a piccolo?"

I took her hand and led her into the kitchen. "I think this is better explained over a glass of wine."

I took a bottle of California chardonnay from the refrigerator and opened the screw cap. Jenny took two wine glasses from the cupboard. We sat on cracked vinyl chairs at the Formica table that I'd acquired at a garage sale the week I moved to Two Harbors. The entire house was furnished in garage sale or hand-me-down furniture that fit my Whistling Pines salary. The wine glasses were cut-glass lead crystal, a bargain acquired at an estate sale, and the only matching pieces of glassware in my kitchen. Jenny neatly arranged the pile of music to make space for the glasses and wine bottle.

"Dolores has a black toe and she was trying to take a picture of it with her cell phone. It seems that the doctor doesn't charge for e-mail messages but she has the Medicare co-pay for office visits. After I took the picture, she gave me the piccolo."

"If Dolores had the piccolo, I assume that it's high quality."

"I'm not an expert," I replied. "But it's sterling silver and it must be valuable," I said as I opened the case and assembled the pieces. I showed her the Gemeinhardt logo and sterling silver markings.

"Can you play a piccolo?"

"Maybe."

She sipped her wine and leafed through the stack of music as I returned the piccolo to the case. "Can you get familiar with this music before tomorrow night?" She looked up at me and back at the stack.

"I should be able to skim the music and not embarrass myself. It'd be better if I could spend the day working through it on the piano..."

"Except that you have to deliver a van full of senior citizens to the fair in the morning and then you promised to go to the fair with Jeremy and me tomorrow afternoon. That leaves almost no time before the evening concert."

"Like I said, I can skim the music and probably not embarrass myself."

Jenny sipped her wine and looked back to the stack. "I suppose I should finish my wine and go home so you can do your skimming tonight."

I reached across the table and squeezed her hand. "I can skim it in the morning before I go to work. After all, what's the worst they can do if I screw up? Fire me?"

Chapter 11

Saturday morning

I woke to tingling in my right hand. When my eyes opened I saw that Jenny's head was resting in the crook of my elbow. Her blonde hair was jumbled and her face looked as if it was porcelain, spider-webbed with tiny blue veins. The sheet was pulled to her chin and her right knee was resting on my thigh, her arm across my chest. When I shifted, her skin stuck to mine and her eyes fluttered open.

"Are you getting up?" she asked.

"I need to pee," I said, lifting her arm from my chest and shifting to the edge of the bed.

"Not the most romantic opening line I've heard," she replied.

I rolled back and cupped her chin in my hand and kissed her gently. "I'll be right back."

"You may want to brush the fur off your teeth if you expect me to be friendly," she said to my back as I scooted across the cool hardwood floor to the bathroom.

On the way back to bed I closed the bedroom window and then I slipped under the covers. I was chilled, the overnight temperature having dipped into the 60s and I'd turned off the furnace for the summer, leaving the bedroom temperature only slightly warmer than outside. I pulled the comforter over us. Jenny recoiled from my goosebump covered legs.

"Stay on your own side until you generate some body heat," she said, retreating to the far edge of the double bed and holding me at arm's length.

I swept her hand aside and pulled her close. She shrieked in response, which led to a wrestling match under the covers, and eventually to a long kiss.

"Is the piccolo in your pocket?" she asked playfully.

"I'm not wearing pants."

Chapter 12

The residents were lining up for the van when I brought the sign-up sheet from my office. Wendy pulled the van under the portico and was helping load a scooter onto the hydraulic lift as I checked names off the list. Once everyone was loaded I was left standing with Ann Micres Allen, one of the volunteer chaperones. Her father, Ted Micres, was on the list, but nowhere in sight.

"I haven't seen your father this morning," I said to Ann.

"I spoke with him on the phone just before I left home," she replied. "He was excited about going to the fair."

We were interrupted by Howard Johnson who was pointing to the parking lot. "I think Ted decided to drive himself," Howard said, pointing to a vintage, rusty Oldsmobile 88. One of its back wheels was hung up on a concrete barrier.

Ann and I walked to the car. The rear wheel off the ground was spinning. Ann knocked on the window and when Ted saw her face he floored the accelerator, making the engine race and the wheel spin even faster. He was hunched over the steering wheel as if he was racing down the road. Ann knocked again and he seemed surprised to see her still standing next to him. He looked at the speedometer and kept the engine racing. I opened the door and reached in, noting the speedometer reading of 135 mph before I shut off the engine and took the keys out of the ignition.

"Ted, where are you going?" I asked as I handed the keys to his daughter.

"I'm driving to the fair!"

"But you signed up to take the van," I said. I gently took his arms and helped him stand.

"Why would I take the van when I can drive myself?"

Ann pocketed the keys and took her father by the elbow. "Dad, the doctor says you can't drive anymore. Where did you find the car keys?"

"I lost the other set, but I always keep a spare set in my handkerchief box."

"Are there any other sets in your apartment?" she asked as she helped him up the van step.

"I'll have to check my toolbox. I might have another spare there," Ted replied.

After Ted was safely seated Ann shook her head. "I took two sets of keys out of his apartment after he blacked out last month. I told him he couldn't drive anymore, but I had no idea he had more keys." She hesitated, then said, "Can I leave the car where it is for now? I'll get it towed to my brother's house. My nephew just got his license and this might be the perfect vehicle for him to drive around town."

With Ted's turmoil behind us, I spent the morning walking the fairgrounds with Abigail (Abby) Brown and Peggy (Ski) Ziminski. They're both mobile and it was an easy walk with two of the more lucid and funny residents. It left me in good spirits, and when I emptied the van at Whistling Pines I was looking forward to my fourth trip to the fair, this time with Jenny and Jeremy.

When I met Jenny at the gate Jeremy was already wired. "Let's start at the midway 'cause I want to go on every ride at least twice!" He raced ahead while Jenny and I followed, holding hands.

By the time we got to the booth that sold wristbands for unlimited rides, Jeremy had linked up with two of his friends. The three boys were in awe of the dozen fair rides set up on the small fairgrounds and were plotting the sequence of rides and food for their afternoon at the fair. Jeremy raced back to Jenny, who was reaching for her wallet before he got to us.

"Um, Mom, could you guys kinda disappear for a while?" Jeremy asked, looking over his shoulder to make sure his buddies didn't see him talking with his mother. "I could buy a wristband and meet you somewhere later."

Most places in the world, a mother's mental alarms would be clanging if her young son asked to traverse the fairgrounds with his buddies. Two Harbors isn't like most of the world. Daytime crime is so rare, Jenny had no qualms about setting Jeremy loose with his friends for the afternoon.

As we walked away, I said, "You know he'll be on a sugar high for the rest of the weekend."

"I doubt it," she replied. "Those three will go a few rounds on the Tilt-A-Whirl and they'll be tossing their cookies into a garbage can before we go home."

"So, your role in this is to bankroll the trip and stay out of sight?" I asked.

Jenny smiled. "I've heard it only gets worse as they get older." She steered me to the Lutheran church lunch counter. "I missed lunch. Let's grab something to eat and get out of the sun for a while."

We walked into the Lutheran Lunch Counter, housed inside the steel-sided building that looked like a barn with picnic tables. I ordered a cup of coffee and a slice of apple pie. Jenny ordered a Cobb salad. The woman who took our order had a round face and a big smile. She wore a hairnet and a white apron stained with ketchup and mustard. The aroma of grilling onions and French fries filled the space

"Are you getting nervous about your directorial debut?" she asked as we sat at a picnic table. We were between mealtimes and most of the tables were empty.

"I've been too busy to think about it since I leafed through the music over coffee," I replied. "But thanks for bringing it back to the surface."

She smiled as she tore open a packet of low-fat French dressing and drizzled it over the salad. "My mom and dad will be here in an hour. I assume you forgot to invite your mother."

"Dang it," I said with feigned distress. "It slipped my mind."

"Not to worry," Jenny said. "My mother called your mother and told her about the concert and suggested we have dinner together afterward. Mom said Audrey sounded very excited."

"You know I don't see this going well. I can't imagine people more polar opposite than our parents. Just try to make sure the conversation steers clear of politics. Luckily, there isn't an election until November."

"I think they're all polite enough to respect each other," Jenny said as she sliced up her salad, evenly distributing the toppings.

"Mother isn't known for her tact. Now I can worry about the concert *and* the tempest at dinner to follow. Life could hardly be better," I groaned.

"The concert will be fine," Jenny said. "I'm sure the musicians are professional and they'll perform well regardless of the change of director."

"Great! You're trying to make me feel better, but now I feel useless. I suppose the band could play with a trained monkey holding the baton."

I felt the picnic table shift and turned to see a middle-aged man dressed in a while golf shirt and black shorts. He carried a black musician's case and had an enormous walking cast on one foot.

"I'm John Carr," he said, offering his hand. "I'd like to think I'm more than a trained monkey when I'm conducting the band."

I shook his hand and tried to find some words to explain my flippant comment, but he cut me off. "Don't worry. The band is very experienced and the director's job is mostly to make sure we're all playing the same song and start at the same time."

"What happened to your foot?" Jenny asked.

John squirmed. "I won't admit this to many people, but I broke my heel jumping off Ilgen Falls. I'd done it a thousand times as a kid and I was there with my wife watching a bunch of teenagers jumping in. Well, it just got kind of crazy from there. The kids dared me. Let's just say my wife isn't pleased with me."

"You jumped off Ilgen Falls?" Jenny asked, briefly looking at the gray in his hair and trying to guess his age.

"It's not the craziest thing I've ever done, but it ranks near the top of the list *and* it was a double-dare!"

"You seem like such a buttoned-down guy," I said. "What tops the list?"

"I have this really crazy friend named Albee. When we were teenagers, we dared each other to jump off the ore docks into Lake Superior."

"You jumped off the ore docks?" Jenny asked, somewhat in shock. I tried to envision the height of the docks, where the big ore boats are loaded with taconite pellets, and guessed they were two hundred feet above the water. "That's like cliff diving in Mexico."

"We never made it onto the docks. We climbed the security fence and were sneaking onto the docks when a railroad guy saw us and chased us away. Even though Albee is sad we never made the jump, just planning the attempt still ranks at the top of my list of questionable actions.

Albee still gives me a bad time about being the one who chickened out." He paused, then added, "That's probably just ahead of the time Roger "A-Bomb" Anderson and I mixed fuel oil with fertilizer. We set off an explosion in a woodpile that cracked windows in the Catholic Church and rained splinters over half the town."

I looked at the instrument case he'd placed on the table and sized it up. "You're playing alto sax tonight?"

"The doctor said I shouldn't lift anything, so I figured I should stick with the alto rather than the baritone sax until I get out of the cast."

"Hopefully, you'll be well-enough mended to direct the band again next spring," Jenny said.

"That should be no problem, although I am building a zip line course for my kids and it looks pretty tempting," he said with a smile. He used my shoulder to lift himself up from the picnic bench and picked up the saxophone case. "I'll see you in a couple hours under the tent." He stood and lifted his cast, "I'd say 'Break a leg,' but somehow that seems inappropriate."

"John's an interesting guy," Jenny commented as he walked away. "Somehow I had expected the band director to be more of a milquetoast person than someone who'd jump off the ore docks on a dare."

"Musicians are pretty diverse and many of them are out of the mainstream, some further than others," I said. "Back in the Roaring Twenties professional musicians were the bad boys of entertainment and because of the hours playing evening concerts and then the time required to emotionally wind down afterwards, they resorted to a mixture of alcohol and drugs to be awake for concerts and to fall asleep later.

"That didn't end with prohibition. Think of all the craziness at Woodstock and the whole Haight-Asbury music and drug scene. I guess I'll withdraw my earlier comments, but it just seems like the Two Harbors' band shouldn't be part of the craziness. They're all local folks who are going to school or holding down jobs and are pretty well woven into the community.

"Based on what the tuba player told me, the trombonists and tubists are all nutty and take great pleasure in irritating the rest of the band members. There's at least one man, or woman, who's in the midst of sex reassignment, and one bassoon player who irritates the others by skipping practices, showing up late for performances, and dressing provocatively."

We watched Jeremy rush to the door of the food building and scan the dark interior, looking for us. He hurried to our table and said, "I need some more money." His shirt was already stained with chocolate, ketchup and mustard.

Jenny fished a five dollar bill from her fanny pack and held it out. "This means you'll have to take the garbage out the rest of the summer, when asked, and without complaint."

"OK," he replied as he snatched the bill from her hand.

Chapter 13

Saturday, late afternoon

Dozens of musicians were talking and assembling their instruments behind the bandstand. Each nodded politely as I passed. I shook a few hands and accepted the well wishes of the three flutists, who ranged in age from twelve to sixty. As expected, the official warm-weather band uniform was white shirts over black slacks, but the variety was endless, from the virtuoso 8th grade clarinetist, who wore a white Hanes t-shirt over black biker shorts, to an octogenarian French horn player in his starched white shirt with a red bow tie under a handsome black suit. With the temperature approaching 80 degrees, I was already sweating in my white golf shirt and hoped I wouldn't end the evening by falling into the French horns with heat stroke.

Brian Johnson was removing his tuba from its huge case. He was dressed in a black polo shirt and white shorts, the opposite arrangement of everyone else. "Do you have any words of wisdom for me before I screw up this event?" I asked.

"You're already halfway there."

"I am?"

"You're wearing dark pants so no one will know if you wet yourself," he said with a smile.

"Tuba humor," I said, feeling my tension break.

"That's what we're best at." He inserted the mouthpiece and blew a few deep resonant notes and then ran up and down a scale. "Still works."

"Anything that I should expect, but don't know enough to ask about?"

He cocked his head and thought. "I guess there are a couple things you might want to keep in mind. "Keep an eye on Keith, the third trombone. He likes to push Ray Hopkins' toupee with his slide."

"You're kidding?" I asked.

"It happens at almost every concert."

"I'm a little concerned about the French horn player in the suit," I said, nodding toward the octogenarian with the bow tie.

"Don't worry about Frankie," Brian said. "He has bad circulation and wears long johns all summer. He's also very classy and takes the band very seriously."

"You're dangling a hint that there are others who are less serious."

"How many tuba players does it take to change a light bulb?" he asked. "Three: One to hold the bulb and two to drink until the room spins."

"Anything serious that needs preparation?" I asked, grinning but shaking my head.

Brian leaned to look past me and nodded to someone. I turned in time to shake hands with a musician about my height with blonde hair tied in a ponytail and a white polo shirt that was stretched tightly over surgically enhanced breasts and black shorts.

"You must be the new conductor. I'm Jessie Bowden," she said, shaking my hand with a firm grip. As Brian had warned, Jessie was in the process of undergoing a sex reassignment and his/her appearance was a blend of strong male facial features and a somewhat deep voice and overly enhanced breasts and female mannerisms.

"I'm pleased to meet you," I said.

"Everyone says you're a very talented musician," Jessie replied. "I hope you decide to continue with the band after John recuperates."

"Thank you."

As Jessie walked onto the bandstand I asked if there would be any other surprises.

Brian cocked his head again and, after a few seconds, he replied, "Sheila."

"Who's Sheila?" I asked.

"She's the bassoonist. She's attractive, always late, usually dressed formally, and arrogant. I'd guess that all the women in the band hate her and half the men in the band would like to get in her bedroom. The other half of the men are impotent, pre-pubescent, or gay."

"How will I recognize her?" I asked.

"She's the only bassoonist, but you'll know who Sheila is as soon as you see her." He smiled and walked to the back of the bandstand, arranging a stool next to the trombones.

I'd scanned the concert crowd as I walked to the podium but my mother was nowhere in sight. It was easy to pick out Jenny's blond hair. She was sitting with Jeremy and her parents near the center of the crowd and she gave me a million-dollar smile.

The musicians responded with quiet professional attention as I crossed in front of them an put on my best game face, even though sweat was trickling down my back. I mounted the podium and nodded to the oboe player, who played an "A," which the other musicians tuned to. I noted the empty chair between John Carr with his alto sax and the lone oboe player, and wondered if an extra chair had been put onto the bandstand, but then remembered Brian's warning about Sheila. As the tuning note died down, a commotion at the back corner of the bandstand caught my eye. Sheila had arrived.

Sheila had neatly coifed blonde hair and was wearing a black cocktail dress that clung to her well-toned body. Tiny straps were the only things keeping the top from revealing excessive cleavage. While there were many attractive women in Two Harbors, including Jenny, Sheila was in the Hollywood starlet category. The entire band was ready to play when Sheila gave me a pouting smile that said, "I might be late, but you'll forgive me anyway. Won't you?" as she slipped through the seated band members, stepping on toes and wiggling her behind in faces. She held her bassoon high in her left hand; sheet music was tucked under her other arm. Her right hand was clutching several brown pill containers. I hoped the pill containers contained prewetted reeds, and not meds Sheila needed to perform.

I saw several musicians rolling their eyes or shaking their heads. After she tripped on John Carr's walking cast and offered him an apology, she sat in the empty chair next to him and started to arrange her music. As she sat her short dress exposed long, tanned legs. I did the only thing that came to mind. I stalled.

"Ladies and gentlemen, I'm Peter Roberts, the recreation director at Whistling Pines and I have the honor of filling in as the guest director for the Two Harbors City Band tonight." Behind me, I could hear Sheila shuffling her chair and the sound of squeaking as she put her reed in place. After a few more stalling comments I heard a few chirps from the bassoon as Sheila tuned it. When I turned back to the band, Shelia was smiling and Brian Johnson was giving me an "I told you so" look. John Carr gave me a nod of encouragement.

I raised my baton and the musicians' instruments all came to attention. When I made the downstroke a miracle happened, the band played perfectly. My apprehension melted away and I found myself flowing with the music.

When I introduced the second song I saw my mother standing in the back corner of the tent. It was hard not to notice her: She was dressed in her typical caftan that looked like it might've been stolen from the costume room of "Joseph and the Amazing Technicolor Dreamcoat". She waved vigorously, as if I couldn't notice her, which sent her dozens of wrist bangles clanging like a separate percussion section. I gave her a discreet nod and we went on with the concert.

We took a short intermission after six songs and I walked among the musicians, shaking hands and thanking them. As Brian Johnson had told me, they were an amazingly diverse group with ages spanning sixty years and occupations from mining engineers to high school students to commercial fishermen, all bound by their common love of performing instrumental music.

And then there was Sheila. She gushed forward, pressing her hand into mine, egregiously violating my personal space on the crowded bandstand. Up close, I could see the makeup that enhanced her appearance from a distance now showed crow's feet at the corners of her eyes, making me think she was closer to fifty than my initial guess of thirty.

"I am so sorry to be late, but I just lost track of time," she gushed in a breathy Marilyn Monroe voice. "I'm Sheila O'Keefe."

"Peter Roberts," I replied, shaking her hand.

"You are doing a wonderful job, Peter. I'm so pleased you were able to fill in for John on such short notice." She had a way of carrying herself and speaking that made me feel like I was the only person of importance in the world. I broke away from her spell briefly and saw three clarinetists shaking their heads in disgust.

"Thank you. As I told the audience, it's an honor to be asked to direct this fine group. Now, if you will excuse me, I have to check on the tuba player." I pulled myself out of

Sheila's aura and pushed my way back to Brian Johnson, who was laughing, nearly in tears after watching my introduction to Sheila.

"Man, you were lucky to get away with your arm," Brian said quietly. "She hooked onto you like a leech. The look on her face was like she was a mosquito and you were fresh blood."

"I think you're mixing your metaphors," I replied, trying to see who Sheila had locked onto after my escape.

"Hey, I'm a tuba player. We're allowed great latitude in metaphor mixology." Brian stopped and cocked his head. "I heard you're an Iraq war vet. The VFW bartender told Keith you'd been a Navy corpsman. Is that true?"

"I don't have time..."

Brian smiled. "The bartender also said that you were very humble. I like that in a director."

"He said humble?"

Brian shrugged. "You don't wear your stripes."

"You say that like a Marine," I said.

"Two tours in Viet Nam. Two purple hearts. I owe my life to two Navy corpsmen. You guys are almost as crazy as tuba players." The musicians were starting to migrate back to their seats and he gave me a nudge. "Give 'em hell, Doc."

"Doc?" I asked.

"Every corpsman I knew was nicknamed Doc, just like every electrician is Sparky."

Before taking the podium I rechecked the crowd. Jeremy had a puff of pink cotton candy, and Jenny gave me thumbs up. Mother had found a chair in the back and was gabbing with the stranger seated next to her, waving her arms to accentuate whatever topic she was spouting upon.

The second half of the concert flew by. The songs were familiar and the musicians were surprisingly talented. Everyone onstage seemed to be in the groove except Sheila. As we got to the last song she seemed fidgety and distressed. I tried not to notice, but she rubbed at her throat and chest and she stopped playing before the song ended. She started gathering her music during the last few bars of the song, which was very distracting for the rest of the band. I wondered if this was all part of her routine: Arrive late and leave early. She was pushing her way off the bandstand before the last notes stopped resonating. I thought she might be having some kind of medical distress, perhaps dehydration or heat stroke.

When the concert ended and I had shaken hands with the musicians, Jeremy, Jenny, and her parents discreetly approached the bandstand. My mother pushed her way through the departing crowd with the subtlety of a grizzly chasing a salmon.

"Peter! Peter!" Mother cried, as if I were about to slip away without noticing her. I waved discreetly in hope that she might slow the onslaught before she bowled someone over. By the time she reached us she was breathless.

"Oh Peter," she gasped. "I was afraid that you were going to exit with the orchestra." She embraced me in a smothering hug and then stepped back as if to inspect me.

"Mother, while you catch your breath, I'd like to introduce Jenny, and her parents, Barbara and Howard Chapman."

"Oh, I finally get to meet your little friend Jenny," Mother said, quickly sizing up Jenny, then giving her a bear hug. Mom whispered something in Jenny's ear that resulted in Jenny turning bright red. As mother stepped back she said, "Please call me Audrey."

After releasing Jenny she caught a glimpse of Jeremy, who was peeking around Howard, apparently trying to evade the hugging scene.

"The person hiding behind Howard is Jeremy, Jenny's son."

Mother reached out to hug Barbara, who quickly engaged the two extended hands and turned it into a two-handed shake. Barbara managed a Mona Lisa smile that nearly cracked her makeup and said, “It’s very nice to meet you.”

Mother, oblivious to Barbara’s hint that Jenny’s family might not be the hugging type, grabbed Howard before he had the chance to dodge her. Mother engulfed him in a hug while he held his arms away from her and gave me a pleading look.

“Mom, I think it’s time to decide where to eat supper.”

Audrey released Howard and quickly scanned the area for Jeremy. Not wanting any part of the hugs, Jeremy had slipped into a row of folding chairs twenty feet away. He looked like a baseball player getting ready to steal second base with his feet spread wide, ready to dart any direction that would take him away from Mother.

“Jeremy, I won’t hurt you. I just want to give you a hug.”

Jeremy shook his head, backed up and tumbled over a chair. He quickly recovered and moved further down the aisle.

From outside the tent I heard a commotion and saw a group of people gathering near the back of the bandstand. I heard someone yell, “Call 9-1-1. We need an ambulance!” and I ran to the gathering crowd.

Sheila was on the ground gasping for air, her bassoon case and open purse were next to her. Several brown pill bottles were strewn near the bassoon case. She was trying to grasp her purse as I pushed my way through the crowd and knelt next to her.

“EpiPen,” she whispered hoarsely.

I ripped her purse open and rifled through the assorted toiletries, makeup, keys, and writing pens until I found the autoinjector pen filled with epinephrine, used to treat severe allergic reactions. “What allergies do you have I asked?” as I flipped the cap off the pen.”

"Nuts," she croaked.

I jabbed the pen into her thigh and held it in place to make sure the enclosed spring-loaded syringe administered the full dose of medicine into her system. "Did someone call an ambulance?" I yelled to the crowd.

"They're coming," a male voice responded from the rear.

Sheila continued having breathing problems. I had nothing else to offer except soothing words that I hoped were encouraging. Jenny pushed in next to me and took Sheila's pulse.

"Sheila has a nut allergy and I injected her EpiPen," I explained.

Jenny picked up the autoinjector and inspected it. "This expired a year ago and it's only a 300 microgram dose. Sheila, is there another EpiPen in your purse?"

I again rummaged through the contents of Sheila's purse, but didn't find another pen. Sheila was shaking her head, apparently unable to speak. She didn't have another pen.

"Does anyone have an EpiPen?" Jenny asked the crowd. Sheila was in severe respiratory distress, her lips were swelling, and she was struggling to draw a breath as her throat swelled. There was no response to the EpiPen request from the accumulated crowd and it appeared that Sheila's expired pen wasn't giving her any relief. I could hear a siren whine nearby.

"Have you ever done an emergency tracheostomy?" Jenny whispered in my ear. "If her throat continues to swell she'll die if we don't open her trachea. I've never even seen one performed except on television."

I flashed back to a scene of carnage in Iraq. On my first mission, an IED exploded throwing a Marine against the Humvee steering wheel, crushing his larynx. I'd pulled him from the scene and done the tracheostomy as he passed out. It was my baptism under fire. Sheila was gasping for air and I prayed she would continue to get enough oxygen to stay lucid.

"Coming through!" I heard the shout from the outskirts of the crowd. Len Rentz, the police chief, opened a lane through the onlookers, leading an EMT who was carrying an oxygen bottle and green face mask.

Jenny assisted the EMT by putting a green plastic mask over Sheila's nose, while explaining that we'd injected an EpiPen. Sheila didn't respond to the treatment and her breathing became increasingly labored. I let Jenny and the EMT take over, gathering the contents of Sheila's purse from the ground and repacking them. I heard the rattle of a gurney rolling over the rough ground and saw the second EMT and a deputy sheriff push through the crowd. Within moments Sheila was strapped to the gurney and rolling toward the ambulance.

Jenny and I were drenched with sweat as we picked up Sheila's purse, the pill bottles, and bassoon case. Len Rentz was at my side.

"What happened?" Len asked.

"Sheila appeared to have an allergic reaction," I replied. "She said she has a nut allergy."

"Allergic reactions like that can come on very quickly," Jenny said. "She's been performing for almost an hour. I think that she must've eaten a nut during the concert."

Len looked around the immediate area and within 100 feet there were three vendors selling roasted peanuts, nut-covered caramel apples, and funnel cakes probably fried in peanut oil. "Looks like there are plenty of places she could've contacted nuts."

"But she knew she had an allergy," Jenny said. "She wouldn't eat something like that on purpose. She must've had a serious reaction sometime in the past to get a prescription for an EpiPen, and anyone with a serious allergy becomes paranoid about their food choices and even preparation.

After what I sometimes called a "blinding flash of the obvious," I set the bassoon case on the ground and opened it, searching for the vials with the wetted reeds. I found all three pill bottles/reed cases and opened the first, pouring out the reed and clear water into my hand. The second didn't have a reed, but as I poured out the water half a peanut tumbled from the vial. The reed from that case was obviously the one still on the bassoon's metal crook.

"Peter! If you suspected that someone had dropped a peanut into the pill bottle, why did you pick it up and get your fingerprints all over the surface?" Len scolded. He pulled a pair of blue surgical gloves from a pocket and slipped them on before taking the bottle and peanut from me.

I felt the red creeping up my face. "Sorry. It was just a hunch and I wanted to check it out."

"See if the musicians are around," he said. "I'd like to talk to them. Maybe one of them saw someone messing with the bottles."

My mother, never the shrinking violet, pushed past Len and looked at us. I became aware of my sweat-stained shirt and the grass and gravel ground into the knees of my pants. "Peter! How do you expect to eat at a nice restaurant dressed like that?"

"Peter just saved a woman's life," Jenny said quietly.

Mother looked at her, noting her sweaty cotton blouse and the sand on her knees. "Well, did he have to be so messy doing it?"

Jeremy pushed past Jenny's parents and sidled next to Jenny. He gave me a knowing look and said, "It was just like when you took the gun away from the crazy woman who was shooting at us! Cool! You just run to where the trouble is and take care of it."

I could see that I'd won a few points with Jeremy, but Mother wasn't persuaded.

"Peter is always getting himself in the middle of something and I'm afraid he sometimes just doesn't show due consideration for others. I'm afraid our dinner plans are ruined." As she spoke, she was gesturing wildly, making the bangles on her wrists sound like a bunch of cymbals. Len, who I've known for years, was straining to keep a straight face.

"I have a clean shirt in the car," I said. "I'll change on the way to the restaurant."

"Is it the hideous Hawaiian shirt you wore to the funeral last spring?" Len asked, trying to add fuel to the fire.

I closed my eyes and waited for the next eruption from Mother. The shirt was indeed a Hawaiian style shirt, but was more seasonally correct now than at the spring funeral and probably coordinated with Mother's multi-colored caftan.

"Peter wore a Hawaiian shirt to a funeral?" Mother asked.

I steered her toward the parking lot. "I broke my nose right before the van left for the funeral and I had blood all over my white shirt, so Wendy, the girl who has the band I spoke about, loaned me a Hawaiian shirt she'd worn to a Luau-themed party." I continued the story all the way to the parking lot where everyone dispersed to their cars.

At the edge of the parking lot we stopped to make plans. "We'll eat at Nokomis, that restaurant on the road to Duluth," Mother announced. "They have a nice menu and it will be halfway to my house. Would anyone like to ride in the convertible with me?" Jeremy raced off to ride with my mother in her red Cadillac convertible and Jenny's parents walked to their Buick.

I pulled the sweaty golf shirt over my head and mopped my face with it as Jenny took the Hawaiian shirt off the hanger in the back seat of my old Corolla. Jenny gave me a hug after the shirt was on and stretched up to kiss me.

"The concert was really good."

"Thanks. The musicians are great and I'm really pleased they asked me to conduct."

"Do you know what your mother asked me?" Jenny asked as we got in the car.

"Well you blushed, so it had to be something very personal. Let's see, did she ask if you were really blonde?"

"Worse."

I shuddered at the thought that Mother would ask my girlfriend something even more tasteless than if her hair color was natural. "I give up. What did she ask?"

Jenny faced away from me and looked out the side window. "She asked what type of birth control I'm using."

"She really asked that?" I almost shouted, knowing full well that Mother's mental filter didn't stop a lot of nosiness.

Jenny nodded assent.

Chapter 14

The Nokomis restaurant, overlooking Lake Superior and located between Two Harbors and Duluth, was above my budget. We followed the convertible with Jeremy in the passenger seat with the bill of his cap facing backwards. Every time he looked back at us he had an ear-to-ear grin.

Despite the lovely view of the lake, dinner was a nightmare. My mother talked endlessly about her charity work. Jenny's mother listened politely and nodded at appropriate points in the conversation. Jeremy talked about riding in the convertible, with the top down, and suggested that everyone in the family get one just like it. He also regaled my mother with the story of the crazy woman who lives next door to me who tried to shoot rabbits from her back porch. Mother thought he was fabricating a tale and no one argued the point. Jenny was still trying to figure out the whole issue of Mother's question about contraceptives.

A huge argument broke out when the check arrived. Mother scooped the folio out of the waiter's hand and jammed her AmEx card into it before anyone could react. Jenny's father tried to intercept the waiter, but mother made such a scene, as only she can, that his Scandinavian predisposition to avoid arguments at all costs overrode his generosity, so he let mother pay, but was obviously smoldering. Mother was oblivious to his displeasure and went on with her discussion about raising funds for an endowed chair at the University of Minnesota Medical School to study post-traumatic stress disorders in returning Iraq war veterans, an issue that had been in the headlines since the first Iraq war.

"You know, it's something that might help Peter, if he'd ever admit he has PTSD," Jenny said. I almost choked on my last bite of cheesecake.

Jenny's father turned and asked, "You were in Iraq?"

Mother started to expound on the number of Iraq war vets with PTSD, apparently not picking up on Jenny's comments, when Jenny did something terribly out of character. She put her hand on mother's arm and raised her finger. Mother sat frozen.

"Daddy, Peter was a Navy corpsman in Iraq. He was wounded and was awarded a Purple Heart, and Bronze and Silver Stars for bravery."

Mother's eyes shot to me and her mouth fell open. She had never asked what I'd done in the Navy. She'd been too busy with her own projects to inquire about my military experience and probably assumed I'd been floating the oceans of the world on a ship. Jenny's father was seated across from me and when he stood, I wasn't sure if he was going to walk out or punch me. Instead he reached across the table and shook my hand.

"Thank you," he said. "This country owes a great deal to people like you."

Jeremy whooped, "Peter's a hero!" which turned heads at neighboring tables.

I turned red, excused myself, and escaped to the restroom. Inside, I leaned against the cool wall tile and closed my eyes. A toilet flushed and I jumped, seeing a Humvee rolled on its back like a turtle. Memories of injured Marines and endless dusty roads with danger in every rock pile flowed freely. Memories I'd buried and hoped to never see again spilled out as the occupant of the toilet stall washed his hands and dried them.

"Are you OK, son?" I opened my eyes to a white-haired gentleman looking at me with concern.

"I'm fine. I just had a little surprise," I said. He nodded and walked out.

A second later I heard the creak of the restroom door and a quiet voice asked, "Peter, are you OK?" Jenny's father was standing inside the door.

"Just catching my breath," I said, taking a deep breath and straightening up.

"I have to say, I owe you an apology."

"Why?" I asked.

"I thought you were this big, dopey, guitar-toting hippie who was taking advantage of my daughter." He stopped for a few seconds, considered his words, and added, "I guess I couldn't have been more wrong. Will you forgive me?"

"I don't think you need to apologize," I replied. "I've been living in my own little world and I hadn't considered what impression I was leaving with you and Barbara."

"Jeremy thinks the world of you," he said with a smile. "Maybe I should've trusted his judgment more than mine."

He took my elbow and steered me out the door. Sensing that my military past was causing problems for me, he changed the topic. "Tell me about your crazy neighbor who was shooting in her backyard. Jeremy said you threw him to the ground and shielded him when you heard the shots."

We talked about the bunny incident as he led me back to the table where everyone was preparing to leave. At the table Jenny's father walked to my mother and hugged her.

"You must be very proud of your son. He's an extraordinary person."

I can never recall a previous time when my mother was speechless.

Jenny walked me to my car and gave me a quick kiss. "I think this went pretty well," she said, holding my hand. "And you were so apprehensive about our parents meeting."

"Well, it's certainly a day I won't soon forget."

"I should ride home with Mom and Dad now," she said, looking back at our mixed family group who were saying their goodbyes quietly in the parking lot.

"I thought Jeremy had a sleepover and you were spending the night at my house."

Jenny looked at the body language of our parents and Jeremy, then gave me a chaste kiss. "I think I'd better spend the night with my folks."

Chapter 15

Sunday

I was in my tiny office sipping from my first cup of coffee when I caught the scent of pipe tobacco. I didn't need to turn to know who was at the door. "Hi Len," I said.

"Once again you ran to the emergency and came through," he said, pulling a pipe from his pocket and filling the bowl with Honey Cavendish tobacco.

"What emergency?" I asked.

"Sheila O'Keefe survived her allergic reaction. I talked to her in the hospital this morning and she's going to be released as soon as the doctor makes his rounds. She told me to thank you."

"I'm happy to hear she's bouncing back so quickly," I said.

"She'd like to thank you in person."

I flashed back to Brian Johnson's comments about Sheila's questionable ethics. "I'm sure I'll run into her in town."

Len put the pipe stem in his mouth and patted his pockets, looking for a lighter. "She was very sick when she got to the hospital. The ER doctor said if you hadn't stuck her with the EpiPen there's a good chance she would've died."

"I'm glad she had one in her purse." When Len pulled the lighter from his pocket I added, "You know you can't smoke in here."

Len sighed and put the lighter away. "Sheila also told me that she'd left the reed cases next to her chair during the intermission when she bought a bottle of water so anyone on the stage could have dropped a peanut into the case."

"Somebody who knew she had an allergy wanted to scare her," I said.

"She could've gone into anaphylactic shock and died. The county attorney says he might consider filing a charge of attempted murder."

"It might've been a sick prank gone wrong," I replied feebly, not wanting another murder investigation anywhere near me.

"It might've been put there by someone trying to kill her."

"Why are you telling me?" I asked, with the sinking feeling I knew the answer.

"The doctor said Sheila's peanut allergy is so severe she was exposed to the peanut less than an hour before her collapse."

I quickly did the math while Len waited, knowing he'd piqued my interest. "She came in contact with the peanut during the concert.

My mind was reeling, recalling the mix of musicians shuffling around the crowded bandstand during the intermission. I tried to envision the activity around the area where Sheila had been seated.

"Maybe it fell in by accident," I suggested.

"She capped the reed case. Was anyone from the crowd on the bandstand during the intermission or only the band?" Len asked.

"I don't remember seeing anyone except the band there. It was already crowded with musicians and I can't imagine anyone else coming up there."

"Then I guess our culprit is a musician," Len concluded.

"Len, I know where this discussion is going and I don't know any of the musicians well enough to be of any help."

Len smiled. "I interview people I don't know in every investigation. Why should you be different?"

"The first reason is, I'm not a cop. Secondly, I don't want to be a cop."

"OK, you're not a cop, but you are the best trained witness at the scene of the crime."

"I talked to the tuba player through nearly all of the intermission," I said. "I'm unaware of anything else that happened."

"Great start!" Len said. "We've eliminated the tuba player as the assailant. Who else can we rule out?"

"That's a first," a voice came from behind Len, just before Brian Johnson peeked over Len's shoulder. "The tuba player is always the prime suspect." Brian stuck his hand out and introduced himself to Len. "Hey, do you guys know the range of a tuba? It's about twenty yards if you get a tight-fitting potato." Brian laughed at his own joke. I grimaced.

"Ah, the tuba player," Len said.

Brian handed me a manila folder. "Hi, Doc. I have to run, but here's the music for Thursday's concert."

I grabbed Brian's hand and pulled him into the office. "Close the door, Len."

As Brian and I got past our first uncomfortable exchange, he's loosened up and I thought of him more and more as an interesting and funny guy. During the concert I'd looked back at him swaying along with the rhythm of a waltz with his eyes closed, playing the notes from memory. I could almost envision him in lederhosen and a Tyrolean hat.

"Brian, since we've eliminated you as a suspect in Sheila's incident, I thought we could pick your brain," I said, clearing the one office chair and almost pushing him into it.

"Whoa, Doc!" he exclaimed. "If the hot lights come on, I'm outta here."

"You probably saw that Sheila had a severe allergic reaction and collapsed after the concert last night," Len said

"I saw her on the ground, but I didn't know what was happening," Brian replied. "It looked like Peter and his girlfriend had things under control so I didn't want to stick my head in."

"Sheila's allergic to nuts and someone put a peanut in her reed container," I said

Brian looked back and forth between Len and me, apparently searching for a punch line. "You guys are serious?" he asked.

"She nearly died," Len explained.

"Yikes. I know she rubs a lot of folks the wrong way with her chronic tardiness, but killing her off." Brian shook his head in disbelief. "Well, that's way over the edge."

"Did you see anyone tampering with her reed containers?" Len asked. "They were little brown pill bottles with pop-off white lids."

Brian wrinkled his nose. "You know, I just kinda sit in the back row and let things go by. Sometimes I joke around with the trombones and drummers, but I'm pretty much always in the back row. Peter and I were talking for a while during the break and then I told a couple tuba jokes to the trombone players. Say! How does a tuba player..."

"Not now, Brian," Len said. "Is there someone who's been very angry with Sheila?"

"The whole band is mad at Sheila. She's always late and makes us all wait while she gets settled and tunes. Worst of it is she seems to revel in the attention, even if it's negative."

"Have there been any specific incidents where band members were angry? Anything out of the ordinary?" Len asked.

I saw a twinkle in Brian's eye and braced for another tuba player joke, but he surprised me when he said, "Sheila took Brandy Childer's music stand during the Memorial Day concert so Brandy had to share the second chair music with Sue Kotowski."

"Brian," I said, "I don't think that Brandy would kill Sheila over a music stand."

"I agree, but Len asked if anything out of the ordinary happened. All the other stuff is ordinary. Like I told you, Doc, the clarinets are mad at the trombones and most of the women are jealous of Sheila's appearance. I think most of the band is creeped out about Jessie's sex change. But none of those things are out of the ordinary. When you throw together any group of talented musicians there's always friction. Talented people are...different."

"But they don't kill each other," Len said.

"Not usually," Brian replied. "Can I go now? Doc's office is giving me claustrophobia." He looked around nervously. "Was this a broom closet?"

Len pulled the door open and Brian left with a wave.

"Why does Brian call you Doc?" Len asked.

"He found out I used to be a Navy corpsman and he started calling me Doc."

Len nodded and closed the door. "Do you think Brian is being straight with us?" he asked as he clamped the pipe stem between his teeth and took out the lighter. He waved me off when I started to protest. He lit the pipe, inhaled deeply and blew the smoke at the ceiling vent. I looked at the smoke alarm in the opposite corner and wondered how much smoke was required to trigger the alarm.

"I don't know Brian very well, but he's been straightforward with me. The first time we met, he brought music for the concert and told me he was unhappy because even though he was the backup conductor, I'd been asked to step in. Once he said his piece, he told me what I needed to know and has been very nice. Well, aside from the deluge of corny tuba player jokes."

"I went to high school with his older brother, Mike. I mostly remember Brian as a pesky little brother who wanted to tag along with the big kids. I see him around town occasionally and say 'Hi' but I've never really known him. I know that I've never arrested him or any of his kids, so he can't be too much of a troublemaker."

"Brian warned me about Sheila before the first performance."

"Warned you about what?" Len asked.

"Like he said, Sheila would be late and would be dressed in a way that would irritate the women in the band. I have to say that he was right on all counts based on the number of people I saw rolling their eyes when she came onstage."

"It's interesting he mentioned that the women are most irritated with her," Len said, taking another drag on the pipe. "Poisons are most often a weapon of choice for female murderers and suicides. I'd classify a peanut as a poison to someone with an allergy."

I did a quick mental count and said, "That eliminates the twenty men, about forty percent of the band."

"I wonder how many people knew about Sheila's nut allergy?" Len asked. "Before the HIPAA laws, I would've included anyone who works at a hospital or clinic as likely suspects, but the patient privacy laws have really put a clamp on the amount of patient information that's accessible to medical personnel."

"I don't know, Len. She could've declined nuts at a party or bar, mentioning her allergy. Or it could be a waiter at a restaurant where she made sure there were no peanuts in her Kung Pao chicken."

"Are there any waitresses or nurses in the band?" Len asked.

"I have no idea. I've only conducted them once and I don't know the names of more than a handful of them."

"The season-ending concert is next Thursday in the bandshell. That gives you four days before the concert to check it out," he said as he tucked his pipe away and walked out the door.

"Why am I checking it out?" I yelled after him. "You're the detective!"

Wendy swept in on Len's heels. "I smell tobacco smoke!"

Wendy is a militantly anti-smoking and shows up unexpectedly at inconvenient times. This was an inconvenient time for her to appear.

"Len Rentz just left. It's not a big deal," I said.

"It is a big deal! Second-hand smoke kills millions of people a year and is the primary cause of most bladder cancer. It's also against the law to smoke inside a public building. You are abetting him!" Her round face was turning red and she was shaking a rolled up newspaper at me as if I were a misbehaving dog.

"Len's gone. I'll remind him if he comes back. I got it, no smoking. It's the law."

Wendy lost her head of steam and said, "All right." She unfolded the newspaper and flattened it, showing me the crossword puzzle. "The clue for 34-across is, 'A drawer in a drawer.' The answer is nine letters long."

"Underwear," I said.

She counted off the spaces and then looked at me skeptically. "Have you already done the crossword today?"

"No. I don't do crosswords."

She leaned against the door and filled the letters in the spaces. She tapped her pencil on the paper a couple of times and said, "It seems to fit."

I shrugged. "OK. Is there something else you wanted?"

"No. That was pretty much it." She turned and left.

A little headache started creeping up my forehead and I realized I hadn't met my daily dose of caffeine. I walked through the dining room, now quiet between breakfast and lunch, and drew a cup of coffee from the urn on a counter. I sipped my coffee and looked at the spectacular view. The large dining room windows overlooked the green lawn that fell away like an infinity pool to the cobalt blue of Lake Superior. A mile or two from shore a ship plowed through the cold water on its way to pick up taconite pellets in Duluth. The ship was so far off it was hard to tell it was making headway.

There'd been a newspaper article the previous week about a kid who jumped into the Duluth ship canal on a dare and was so cold he couldn't swim to the ladders spaced along the length of the canal. He'd been lucky because a fisherman pulled him out of the water before he slipped under the cold water. I flashed back to John Carr's story about Albee daring him to jump off the ore loading docks, and wondered if either of them would be alive if they'd actually made the jump. If the fall hadn't killed them, I wonder if they could have made it to shore before they were overcome by hypothermia. They might never have been found. As Gordon Lightfoot sang in "The Wreck of the Edmund Fitzgerald" the big lake never gives up her dead.

"Peter, are you daydreaming?"

I turned and found Miriam Milam approaching with a tray. I like Miriam. I find her witty and smart and I am amazed by her boundless energy and compassion. Whenever anyone was sick or had a personal tragedy Miriam would buy a card and track down every member of the staff to get their signature.

"I hear you're working with Len to see who poisoned that woman in the City Band," she said as she quickly set the salt and pepper on each table.

"The rumor mill must be broken," I said. "She wasn't poisoned. She had an allergic reaction."

Miriam stopped and cocked her head. "Someone said that she was flopping like a bass."

"Are we having a conversation, or are you pumping me for information?"

"Hard to say," she said as she went back to setting out the salt and pepper. "I heard you were giving her mouth-to-mouth." Miriam peeked over her shoulder to see how I reacted.

"Do you know Sheila O'Keefe?" I asked.

"I've run into her a few times. Can't say I really know her," Miriam said, finishing her task and drawing a cup of coffee. "Why do you ask?"

"I'm just curious. She was the woman with the allergic reaction and I was wondering how many people knew about her allergy to nuts."

Miriam took a sip from her cup, obviously contemplating her words. "Sheila is pretty well known around town, although not many people are, what you'd call close friends. She's overly friendly sometimes."

"Wow. Sounds like I should've been more careful than to give her mouth-to-mouth."

Miriam's eyes sparkled. "I guess that means Jenny won't have to worry about me stealing you away now that you're soiled goods." She got up and disappeared into the kitchen. I was pretty sure Jenny didn't need to worry about competition from Miriam, who was happily married. She was so busy with a farm and other ventures I'm not sure how she found time to work at Whispering Pines, much less have time for an extramarital fling. I overheard her say once that she needed the job here so she and her husband were covered by medical insurance and to smooth the budgetary ups and downs of a farm income.

I went back to my office and leafed through the sheet music, all marches, for the next concert. I noted a few repeat songs from the fair concert, but most were new. I made a mental note to spend some time looking at the arrangements, then picked up the sign-up sheet for the van of residents going to the final day of the county fair.

The list of residents in need of a ride was shorter. By Sunday, the fair winds down. The ribbons have been awarded in all the 4-H competitions and the people are loading their projects in cars, trucks, and trailers to take them home. The Sunday highlight for many of my retirees is the discounting many food vendors offer so they don't have to cart the food away.

I had six passengers in the van; five were residents, and the sixth was Wendy, who was coming along as the second chaperone. She sat behind me to bug me.

"Peter, tell me about the woman who almost died after the concert," Wendy said, leaning over the rail that separated the driver from the passengers.

"Sheila O'Keefe had an allergic reaction to a peanut."

"I know that," Wendy said, waving her hand as if to sweep that fact away. "I want to know about her. I heard she's a cougar and is particularly attracted to men with wedding rings."

"I can't help you out," I replied. "The first time I met her was at the concert."

"But people must've warned you about her."

I thought back to Brian's warning comments before the concert and my discussion with Miriam this morning. "No, she was pretty much unknown to me before the concert."

"Man, you must live in a bunker somewhere where the sun doesn't shine and gossip doesn't penetrate," Wendy said with a grin.

"I work sixty hours a week, including most of my days off, and spend the rest of the time eating or sleeping. That doesn't leave a lot of time for rumor mongering. Where do you find time to scrape up rumors?"

"Whistling Pines is a great rumor mill with all the old folks sitting around with lots of time to repeat, or improve, rumors. The people who still drive get into town and catch up on the local gossip, then share."

"The barber shop and the beauty parlor," I said.

"They're good, but people only go there every few weeks. I see a lot of little old men sitting around McDonald's in the morning drinking ninety-nine-cent coffee. The women seem to hang out more at The Vanilla Bean."

"Tell me, what do the town gossips say about Sheila O'Keefe?" I asked.

"Like I told you, she's a cougar who likes to chase down younger men."

"Does she hang out in the bars?"

"How would I know?" Wendy asked. "I've never seen her at the places my band plays, but that doesn't mean she's not drinking somewhere else."

It took some time to unload all my passengers at the fairgrounds. Last off was Hulda Packer, who uses a walker to get around Whistling Pines, but is not mobile enough to use the walker at the fairgrounds with uneven ground and longer distances. I lowered her wheelchair from the van using the electronic lift and locked up. Peggy Warren, one of our newer residents, who was able to walk but not drive, walked along with us. The other four residents were all mentally and physically able to move about the fairgrounds by themselves.

"I want to see the 4H building," Hulda blurted out. I'd never seen her hide her opinions or wishes. In some ways, I appreciated her frank input. In other ways, I sometimes wished she'd be quiet and let a few of life's inconveniences pass without comment.

We pushed down a matted grass pathway past a few food vendors and a large building that housed vendors selling anything from Amway products to leaf-free replacement gutters. The aroma of grilling turkey legs and mini-doughnuts filled the air.

"Darn it, Peter," Hulda said. "You could steer around a few of the bumps. This wheelchair doesn't have tension-bar suspenders!"

I grinned at Hulda's mangling of torsion-bar suspension. She had a huge vocabulary, but got the words twisted all the time. "Hulda, I think the phrase is torsion-bar suspension."

"I know! That's what I said!" She blurted in her outdoor voice. "You know, I was married to an engineer who talked about technology like that all the time."

"I didn't know your husband was an engineer," I said as I carefully skirted a rock jutting through the trampled grass.

"He was brilliant!" Hulda said. "He worked in the mines and had five patents for mining drills and devices he'd invented."

"Wow," I said. "I don't think I've ever met anyone who had a patent."

"He was always tinkering with things around the house and in our cars. He took out all the little dashboard warning lights and installed gauges. He wanted to know the oil pressure was low before the idiot light told him he was on the verge of ruining the engine."

"That seems very wise," I said.

"It doesn't work if you've got a station wagon full of screaming kids," Hulda said, waving her arm for emphasis.

"I was busy trying to keep the kids from killing each other but it was my fault I didn't notice the little stinking needle on the stinking little gauge when it went to zero. I didn't notice a stinking thing until the stinking engine seized up and we sat in front of Dunnigan's Pub with a car that wouldn't run.

"And then the engineer came driving up in his fancy pickup truck and had the nerve to point out which gauge I was supposed to watch for oil pressure. One of seven gauges he put in, none of them with labels."

"What did you say?" I asked.

"I told him I was too busy seeing if any of the kids was bleeding or throwing up and I didn't notice a gauge that showed zero. Then he said, 'It doesn't matter which one you're looking at, dear. None of them should be zero!'"

Peggy had been listening silently to the rant until that point. Now curious, she asked, "Did he hook up the idiot lights for you?"

"Hell no! You know what the engineer did? He painted little red zones on the gauges and make little labels for them. Then he took me by my hand and showed me the fancy little gauges and said I should stop the car if any of the needles went into the red zone."

"Did that work for you, Hulda?" Peggy asked.

"I told him if the needles went into the red zone it was because he wasn't taking care of the car. I said it was *not my job* to watch the stinking little needles on the stinking little gauges. My job was to drive the car and keep the kids from killing each other. It was *his job* to make sure the little needles never went into the red."

"Here we are at the 4H building," I said as we rolled up the concrete apron leading into the steel pole barn that housed the 4H exhibits. I was pleased that we could move on to other topics.

We walked down the fiber craft aisle, rolling past hand-tatted doilies, embroidered dishtowels, and pillow covers, braided and hooked rugs, and cross-stitched and crewel-embroidered pictures. I stopped in front of a prize-winning quilt with a triple-purple ribbon dangling from the top edge. The pattern was a sunburst with a yellow center and tiny patches radiating that went from yellow to oranges, to reds, as they got further from the center. I couldn't imagine the hours put into the cutting, arranging and sewing to create a piece of art like I was viewing.

"Whose quilt is this?" Hulda asked.

"The quilter is Arlene Bartlett," I said, reading from a card next to the ribbon emblazoned with the title "Best in Show".

"It looks like all her points match up and end perfectly at the border," Peggy said. "There's not a pucker anywhere and Arlene didn't use any of those appliqués."

"Humph! She wins every year," Hulda said. "The judges should let someone else win once in a while." She pointed to the next quilt and said, "Who is the grand champion?"

I wheeled ahead to the quilt with the single purple ribbon. It was nearly as intricate as the winner, with a patriotic theme involving red, white, and blue pieces sewn in a pattern that looked like a flapping American flag. I marveled at the vision it took to cut and arrange all the pieces in a manner that made the flag look like it was gently waving in a breeze.

"Whose quilt is this?" she asked.

"This one was quilted by Nancy Mohr," I replied.

"I hear she goes to those quilting retreats," Peggy said. "That used to be fun. We'd get a dozen women together and spend a weekend cutting pieces and talking."

"I suppose she won by pandering with that patriotic theme," Hulda grumbled. "Some people will sink to any depth to win."

"Who is the reserve champion, Peter?" Peggy asked.

I wheeled Hulda down to a quilt featuring a bassoon, made from hundreds of pieces of gold and yellow fabric, in the center of the white quilt. Black musical notes were coming out of the instrument, and the white background stitched to look like a piece of sheet music with tiny black notes crossing it.

"Whose quilt is this?" Hulda asked.

I looked at the card next to the pink "Reserve Champion" ribbon and was shocked.

"Peter," Peggy said, "read us the name."

"Sheila O'Keefe quilted this one," I said in amazement.

"Never heard of her," Peggy said, standing close and examining the intricate pieces and the sewing of the reserve champion quilt. "The bassoon and the musical notes are all appliqués. The background sheet music is just machine sewn black thread on a white background. That's much easier than cutting and fitting all the pieces together like Arlene Bartlett does."

She moved to the next quilt, a pretty pattern featuring a clump of purple cone flowers. The stitching was a little rougher and the points on the triangles around the perimeter gapped or were cut short where they met the corners.

"Is this one made by my niece?" she asked. "Her name is Ashley Warren."

I checked the card next to the white honorable mention ribbon. "Yes, this was made by Ashley. She got an honorable mention."

Peggy looked at the quilts winning the first three places and then back at Ashley's piece. "It's a pity that she didn't do better. Only the first three places go to the State Fair and she's been either second or third place for the last five years. She'll be fuming about being snubbed by the judges and her finish doesn't qualify her for the fair." She paused and then added, "Maybe Ashely will take it better than I think. She told me it's a pain in the keister to enter the State Fair competition. You have to make three trips to the fair: One trip to deliver the quilt on the day the fair opens, a second trip to look at all the competitors, and a third to pick it up after the last day of the fair. That's a lot of time and gas money. Either that or you have to spend big bucks to rent a hotel room for the whole ten days and eat all your meals at restaurants or the fair."

"My granddaughter has a quilt here somewhere. Find Lisa Packer's quilt," Hulda requested, ignoring Peggy's comments.

We rolled slowly down the row of quilts, looking at the amazing artistry and talking about the hundreds of hours the quilters had put into their creations and kibitzing about the legality of using one of those fancy sewing machines versus hand sewing all the pieces.

"They should have separate quilting categories," Peggy opined. "It's not fair to put the machine-sewn quilts up against the hand-sewn ones."

After reading dozens of recipe cards with the quilter's name and hometown, I found Lisa Packer's quilt. It was a simple pattern, with six-inch squares of earth tones bordered by a brown strip of fabric. The seams were mostly straight, and obviously hand-sewn. A few of the stitches were puckered. I assumed that Lisa was one of the 4H kids, and this was a really nice effort for a first attempt at quilting. A red ribbon hung from the top edge of the quilt.

"This is Lisa's quilt," I said.

Hulda studied the quilt and asked, "What's that ribbon say?"

"The ribbon says, 'Second Place, Teen 13-18 Home Arts Division.'"

Hulda squirmed in the wheelchair and said, "Well, I suppose she could've won the adult division if they kept those professional quilters out of the competition."

"Hulda, I think Lisa did a wonderful job with her quilt. She should be very proud of herself and her second place ribbon. She can enter it in the State Fair."

We wheeled past the rest of the quilts without comment, my mind going back to the third place quilt, thinking that quilting didn't seem to fit the little I knew of Sheila O'Keefe.

We rolled slowly through the rest of the "Home Arts" exhibits, the garden vegetable and flower exhibits, where the entries were starting to look a little wilted after four days of sitting on tables and stopped in front of a display of home baked breads.

"I baked bread for my family every day," Peggy said, eyeing the loaves, each with a sample slice lying next to the loaf. "These folks make all these fancy shaped loaves with criss-crosscuts on top and weird grains. I made white bread in bread pans, the kind you can make a sandwich from that will keep you full until suppertime."

"Will you look at that!" Hulda said. "They have a category for machine made bread! Why give someone a prize for dumping ingredients into a machine? Ninety percent of the work is kneading the dough to the right texture."

We rolled past canned goods and Hulda pointed to a row of canning jars containing meat. "Look at that, they give prizes for canning venison!" All you do is stick the deer pieces in a jar, cover them with water, and put them in the pressure canner for an hour. Where's the art in that?"

"The trick is not opening the pressure cooker too early," Peggy explained. "Otherwise the jars blow up!"

"That was never a problem at my house," Hulda explained. "The engineer put gauges on everything. We had a gauge on the pressure cooker and he told me never to even think about opening it until the little arrow was at the bottom. We never had an undercooked or overcooked turkey, roast, or chicken because he had little thermometers to stick in them to make sure the temperature was perfect. It was enough to drive a sane person crazy. He always said, 'If there's a way to measure something, I can make a gauge for it!'"

Peggy shook her head. "I wish I'd had someone handy around the house. We had leaking faucets and broken appliances, and my husband couldn't fix anything."

"My husband always said the only things he couldn't fix were broken bones and broken hearts," Hulda replied. "If there was nothing broken in our house he was over helping the neighbors fix a lawnmower or a broken latch on a screen door. He did it all." After a pause she added, "He found out later he couldn't fix his angry wife after he spent a little too much time helping the widow down the block. I nearly had him fixed after that!"

The conversation died abruptly as we rolled over to the mini-donut hut and shared a dozen of the deep-fried, cinnamon-dipped delicacies.

After my experience the first day of the fair, I was reluctant to push Hulda's wheelchair through the barn. As we got near Hulda asked, "Is this where Tinker got injured the other day? Is he out of the hospital yet?"

"Yes, this is where Tinker got bumped by the gate," I said.

"Tinker's back home again," Peggy added. "I saw him at breakfast this morning. You know he was quite a fix-it man around town. That's why everyone calls him Tinker. I called him a couple times to fix things."

I was surprised to hear Tinker was home, considering he was still in the ICU in the most recent report. I looked at Peggy's thick glasses and realized that she could've mistaken almost anyone for Tinker, who was still hospitalized, and would be for a while.

"Show me where he got injured," Hulda demanded before I could correct Peggy.

As we neared the barn we passed a booth with a wood sign that said, "Hand-Made Amish Toys." A young man with a thin blonde beard was packing a box with wooden train cars. Each appeared to be hand carved with small lathe-cut wheels. Behind him was a small table with an array of small hand-made wood toys that looked like guns with a star-shaped wheel atop them.

"Excuse me," I said to the young man. "What are those?" I pointed to the toys with the star-shaped wheel.

"Oh, those are rubber-band guns," he said.

He picked one up and quickly threaded a rubber-band on three star points, then pointed it at a target painted on the tarpaulin at the back of his booth and pulled the trigger three times. Each time he pulled the trigger a rubber-band snapped off the star-wheel, smacked the target, and the wheel advanced, ready for the next shot. He reloaded the wheel and handed it to me. I missed the target with the first rubber-band, then adjusted and struck the target with the remaining two rubber-bands.

"Have you sold many of these?" I asked as Hulda fidgeted in the wheelchair.

He shrugged. "I haven't been in the booth the whole time, but I think we probably sold a dozen or more."

"I'd hazard a guess that you haven't sold one to anyone over sixteen and not one girl bought one."

He smiled. "Thirteen year-old boys are big fans."

"Can we go now?" Hulda asked. "My butt's getting sore. The engineer made a wheelchair cushion for his mother from a piece of foam rubber. That pad saved her from getting butt calluses."

I thanked the man with the rubber-band gun and steered Hulda toward the cattle barn.

"I've never heard of butt calluses," I said.

"You've never been stuck in a chair for months," Hulda retorted. "Your butt calluses up real quick if you don't have a good pad on your chair."

At the barn entrance we were hit with the odors of fresh manure mixed with hay. Many of the stalls were empty now that the judging was complete and the rest of the stalls were full of activity as their occupants prepared to take their livestock home. We passed an empty stall where a young teen was removing the straw bedding with a pitchfork. Further down the aisle we came upon Megan, the freckled red-headed girl who had witnessed Cosmo, the bull, get shot with a rubber-band. She was cleaning her calf pen.

"Hi, Megan," I said, leaning on the pen's railing.

She spun around and looked at me a second before recognition swept her face. She immediately started to blush as she pulled off her leather gloves and picked pieces of straw off her T-shirt and jeans. "Um, you're Peter, with the two old guys."

"I was wondering if you ever figured out who shot Cosmo?"

She looked down at her boots and said, "Uh uh. I gotta clean up. My dad's coming with the trailer to pick up my calf." She spun around and put on her gloves.

"Who bought the rubber-band gun?" I asked, speaking to her back.

"I don't know," she replied without turning.

I looked over my shoulder at the stall across the aisle and a bit further away. Above it hung a Halvorson Farm banner with several ribbons stapled to the bottom.

"Was it one of the Halvorson boys?" I asked.

She turned and looked at me with surprise. She was about to say something when she looked at the banner and hesitated. "You saw their name on the stall."

"What's his name?"

She shook her head and walked to the railing I was leaning on. "I have to go to school with him," she whispered. "I can't tell you who it was." But as she spoke, she discreetly pointed at a blonde boy who was leading a heifer down the aisle.

I winked at her, which made her blush and rush to the back corner of her stall, suddenly interested in something inside the Igloo cooler. I patted Hulda on the arm and said, "I'll be back in a second."

I walked into the unattended Halvorson stall and started lifting the buckets and items stacked on the straw and hay bales in the corner of the stall. I found the rubber-band gun in the pocket of a denim jacket hanging from a nail. "Josh" was written on the label of the coat in a uneven child-like scrawl that would differentiate it from the dozens of other denim jackets at school.

When Josh returned, I was standing in the aisle outside the gate of his stall, the rubber-band gun in my hand.

"Hi Josh," I said holding out the rubber-band gun. "I think this fell out of your jacket pocket."

Josh looked at me skeptically and pushed the gate open. He walked to the jacket and patted the pockets, and then turned back toward me. "When did it fall out?" he asked, holding his hand out, expecting me to give the toy gun back to him.

"I think you lost it right after you shot the bull." I put the gun in my pocket. "If you want it back, it'll be at the sheriff's department. Ask for Deputy Barnes. I'm sure he'd like to take your statement about the incident. A man was injured when you shot the bull."

Josh's eyes grew wide and his mouth dropped open. "I didn't..."

"I was right there," I pointed at a stall past Megan's.

"What are you going to do?" He asked as beads of sweat formed on his forehead.

As I spoke, a middle-aged farmer walked down the aisle and stopped at the stall. "Is anything wrong?" he asked. We exchanged names. He was Josh's dad.

"We have a problem," I said, handing the wooden gun to him. "I was just telling Josh that I think Cosmo, the bull that hurt a man a few days ago, was shot with a rubber-band gun. The shot came from right here and this fell out of Josh's pocket. If you have a piece of paper, write down Hank

Oldham's name. He's in a Duluth hospital with broken ribs from Cosmo's bucking. I'm sure he has an ambulance bill that won't be covered by Medicare, and it would be really nice if someone brought him some flowers to brighten his hospital room."

I turned and walked away, knowing that the punishment meted out from dad would be far worse than any sentence from the court system. I pushed Hulda's wheelchair as I heard Josh being questioned about the Cosmo event. I winked at Megan as I passed, causing another beet-red blush as Josh's father's voice got louder.

"What the hell were you thinking?" I heard Josh's dad say. "Never mind, it's pretty obvious you weren't thinking. When we get home, you're going to write the best apology letter I've ever read, and you won't see the outside of our house or barn until you've earned enough to pay back whatever hospital bills I have to pay..."

"What was that all about?" Hulda asked.

"We just solved a crime and the punishment is being doled out."

Chapter 16

After work on Sunday I drove to my house in the Segog part of Two Harbors. Visions of a cold beer and a pizza sizzling in my oven were swirling through my head. That vision evaporated when I turned the last corner in my neighborhood. My elderly neighbor, Dolores, was standing on my front step holding a basket and pounding her fist on my door.

I pulled into my driveway and got out. "Hello Dolores. What can I do for you?" She was dressed in her usual outfit of a floral decorated dress and black orthopedic shoes that lace to her ankles. Her hair color changed slightly with each trip to the beauty salon. Yesterday it had been battleship gray and today it was mauve.

"I brought dinner for you," she said. "I made a tuna fish hot dish." I learned in the Navy that a hot dish is the Minnesota version of a casserole.

"That's very kind of you," I said as I took the lukewarm pan from her and opened the door. "Would you like to come in and share it with me?"

"No dear. I made it for you because I heard that O'Keefe woman in the City Band died while you were directing and

I assumed that you were in mourning. I always bring a hot dish to people who are in mourning."

"That's very nice, but the woman in the band only had an allergic reaction. She didn't die."

"She didn't die?" Dolores asked. "The ladies at bingo said she'd been stabbed or something."

"No, she had an allergic reaction to a peanut and I'm sure she is recovering nicely."

Dolores looked perplexed. "That O'Keefe woman. Is she the one who wears the sausage dresses?"

"Sausage dresses?" I asked, having a mental image of Lady Gaga who'd worn a dress made of raw meat to some red carpet event. I tried to visualize someone draped in bratwurst.

"Don't be so naïve, Peter. You've seen sausage dresses. The tight ones that make the woman look like she's stuffed into a sausage casing."

"Ah, yes," I said, now remembering Sheila O'Keefe's skintight dress. "Sheila was wearing a sausage dress."

Dolores shook her head. "She's old enough to have grown children. Women like that should dress more properly." She hesitated for a second and then said, "Oh! Well, you keep the hot dish anyway." She turned and started down the steps.

As she limped away I remembered her toe issue and asked, "Did you talk to your doctor about your toe?"

"They don't want to deal with black toes," she said, fluttering her hand at me.

"They may not like to deal with them, but they do," I countered. "What did they offer you for options?"

"The nurse told me to come in, but I'm not about to pay for an office visit over a black toe. The women at bingo told me the doctor would remove it! If they tried to pull that on me I'd give them a piece of my mind. It's been with me for nearly ninety years. It's hardly the time to lop if off, especially when it's only bruised. "

Thoughts of gangrene and blood poisoning flooded through my head and I flashed back to wounded soldiers with flies circling their open bloody wounds. We moved the wounded so quickly to distant hospitals that I never had to deal with the issues associated with black toes.

"If the doctor thinks your toe should be amputated, I would have to agree with him. It looked pretty bad to me."

I got a withering glare. "That doctor is young enough to be my grandson and he hasn't experienced enough to make recommendations about lopping off people's body parts!" With that declaration, she limped back to her house. I thought about asking her to show me the toe, but decided against that plan, at least for the time being. Her limp seemed less pronounced, so maybe it really was a healing bruise and not something more serious.

In the kitchen, I removed the aluminum foil covering the pan and looked at a sickly gray concoction with tiny bits of mushroom showing through a sprinkling of potato chips. It was slightly warmer than the air temperature. Unsure how long it had been stored at that temperature, I decided not to risk food poisoning on the eve of my day off. I slid it into the bag of garbage under the sink and made a mental note to take the bag to the curb for the Monday morning garbage pick-up. I didn't want it incubating in my garbage can.

I had just stocked the refrigerator with a twelve-pack of Lake Superior lager, a specialty beer from a brewery that had moved into the historic Fitger's Brewery building overlooking Lake Superior in Duluth. I twisted the cap off a bottle and took a long swallow, realizing what a long day it had been. I popped a pizza in the oven and leaned back to check the viewing options on the dozen Duluth television channels that came through my UHF antenna and converter. Most evenings I drifted to the PBS stations, except during pledge weeks, which seemed to have gone from annual fund-raisers to monthly. Nothing looked appealing, so I turned to a news broadcast.

I'd nodded off into a dreamless sleep until the doorbell buzzed. I rocketed out of the chair feeling disoriented and panicked I threw myself onto the floor, and blinked a few times before realizing I wasn't reacting to an Iraqi rocket attack. On the television a stupid reality show was following an arguing couple as they raced through a train station trying to find a clue. I took a breath and pushed myself up from the floor and saw Jenny watching me from the open front door.

Her face was pink, like she'd just scrubbed away her makeup. She'd pulled her short blonde hair into a ponytail and was wearing a bright yellow golf shirt with very short denim shorts. The combination caused instant stirring in my loins.

"I wish I could stop doing that," I said, trying to recover my dignity.

I pulled her close and kissed her. "It's a good thing you wear makeup at work. The little old men would be terribly distracted by the beauty you keep hidden underneath."

"That's the nicest compliment you've ever given me," she said, nervously pushing a stray lock of hair behind her ear. She slipped out of my hug and sniffed the air. "Do I smell pizza?"

"I've got a supreme in the oven and the timer should sound any second," I said as I set a scarred aluminum pizza pan on the counter and dug for the slicer in a drawer full of mismatched utensils and soup ladles. On cue, the buzzer sounded, I donned hot pads, and pulled the pizza out of the oven. The cheese was melted and the edges were nicely browned.

"You know," Jenny said as she set two plates on the table, "a good therapist might be able to help you deal with whatever demon makes you throw yourself on the floor when you hear firecrackers or the doorbell."

I ignored her comment, cut the pizza into pieces and slid half a dozen onto two plates as she opened a beer.

"I thought about my mother's work to get a veteran's PTSD treatment center in Duluth and wondered if I should be the first patient," I said as we carried the pizza to the living room and sat on the couch, balancing the plates on our knees. "I'm under control 99 percent of the time and functional. That's an improvement from my return debriefing in San Diego. I'd been a mess, but was trying to keep it buried so I didn't have to go through the mental decompression treatments given to the guys who were obvious basket cases."

"Why did you try to hide it?" she asked as we sat on the couch.

"I don't know," I said, searching for the elusive answer to a question I'd asked myself a hundred times. "I guess it wasn't macho to let your guard down."

"I'm surprised something didn't come out when they did out-processing assessments," she said.

"Somehow I managed to get through the screening and got accepted at the University of Minnesota in Duluth before I'd been scheduled for a discharge. The Navy let me start classes while they finished my out-processing, which allowed me to skip the final round of psych evaluations. I think that's where they might have caught my fragile mental state."

"How did college go?" she asked, getting up and returning from the kitchen with a pair of paper towels that we used as napkins.

"I immersed myself in music theory followed by hours of practicing guitar and piano. By having no downtime I was able to skate through my college days, with Jack Daniels to help me get to sleep. By graduation I was an accomplished musician with a pretty good voice. I was also close to being an alcoholic with night sweats, afraid to close my eyes, knowing that would lead to ugly dreams," I paused, suddenly aware that a line had been crossed. I'd never shared these words with anyone who "hadn't been there."

"What's wrong?" She asked, sensing the pause. She was staring at me, not chewing.

"Just a stray thought," I said. I went on with a new topic. "While my classmates were busy applying for jobs as music teachers I was searching the want ads for something else. I was sitting in the Two Harbors VFW club one Saturday night, talking with a few other vets and trying to explain my dilemma. The bartender, a Viet Nam vet with shaggy gray hair, brought an old, beat-up guitar from behind the bar and handed it to me. 'Play something,' he said."

"Um," Jenny said, trying to swallow. "That would be Vern, the guy who built the box for your medals."

"I spent a few minutes tuning and then played 'Classical Gas,' an instrumental written by Mason Williams, a top 40 hit in the 60s, written by a guy who wrote jokes for the Smothers Brothers Show. When I finished, the bar erupted in applause. I'd closed my eyes and had been so "into" the song that I didn't realize all the conversation had stopped. I nodded thanks to the people and tried to set the guitar aside. Instead, Vern pushed it back to me and I spent two hours playing requests from the crowd. Someone threw my UMD Bulldogs baseball hat on the floor and dollar bills started fluttering in.

"At closing time Vern retrieved the guitar and asked me how I got along with old people. I said I was okay with older people as I gathered the money in my cap and arranged it into a neat pile. He scribbled a name and phone number on a bar napkin and said, 'Call my sister tomorrow.'"

"I thought he was setting up a blind date. I asked why I was calling his sister. He said she was looking for a recreation director. 'She runs some kind of classy apartment thing for retired people up in Two Harbors. She wants someone who can sing and drive folks around in a van.'"

"I wondered how you landed at Whistling Pines."

"My arrival was serendipity," I said, getting up from the table. "Do you want more pizza?"

"I've had plenty," she replied.

"Watching your girlish figure?"

"Mother told me if I didn't watch my girlish figure, the boys wouldn't either."

"I didn't know Barbara was a philosopher."

"Less a philosopher than a narcissist who's consumed with worries about her appearance. She was just passing along wisdom in hopes I'd become as neurotic as she is."

"Ouch."

Jenny shrugged. "It's just the truth as I see it." She sniffed and frowned. "Do I smell fish?"

"Oh heck, I've got to take the garbage out," I said, opening the cabinet and pulling out the waste can. I tied the bag shut, went outside, and threw it in the garbage can. I dragged the can down to the street and returned to the couch.

"I've never known you to cook fish," she said.

"Dolores made a tuna hot dish for me. I threw it in the garbage."

"You don't like tuna?"

"Tuna is fine as long as it's hot or cold. The casserole Dolores brought over was somewhere in between and I had no idea how long it had been out of the oven."

"Good choice."

"I'm surprised to see you tonight. On Sunday evenings you're usually hounding Jeremy about some forgotten homework assignment."

"The strangest thing happened this afternoon. My dad sent Jeremy out to mow the grass and then cornered me in the kitchen. He wanted to know why you'd joined the Navy and what brought you to Two Harbors. When we were through he stared at me for a second, like he was searching for a word."

"He didn't ask you if you were on the pill, did he?"

Jenny punched my arm. "No! Get serious for a minute."

"Okay. I'm serious."

"He apologized for having doubts about my judgment. He told me that he'd apologized to you too, then he asked me if you were having problems with PTSD."

"Why is everyone suddenly concerned about my PTSD?"

"Hang on. I haven't even got to the best part yet. He told me that he'd be proud to have you for a son-in-law."

"I'm not sure what I should do with that tidbit," I said, wondering where the conversation might lead.

"Don't you think it's nice that you have his blessing when you ask to marry me?"

"How'd we get from PTSD to wedding discussions?"

"How are you at catching hints tonight?"

"I think the wedding suggestion was more than a hint."

"Daddy told me he thought you shouldn't have been alone last night after dredging up memories that caused you to flash back, so he told me to come over and comfort you tonight. He and Jeremy are going to Pizza Hut after his homework is done and then he's taking Jeremy down to the lake and showing him how to cast a fly rod."

"That's really nice of him."

She pulled my arm over her shoulders, gave me a gentle kiss, and threw a leg across my lap. "I shaved my legs."

I gently kissed her and ran my fingers up her thigh. She pulled my free hand to her breast.

"Mmm, first and second base in thirty seconds," I said.

"The hit is already out of the ballpark, music man. Take your time with the rest of the bases."

Chapter 17

Monday

I made coffee and thought about my lack of an air conditioner and how hard it was going to be to sleep the next few nights. The weather pattern changed overnight and the Monday morning *Duluth News Tribune* said the westerly winds would bring near-record heat the next three days, not that it had been cool the previous week. Most of the northern hemisphere expects southerly breezes to bring heat, but Two Harbors lies on the north shore of Lake Superior and winds from the south and east are chilled by their trip over the refrigerator-cold waters of the big lake. Winds blowing from the west bring the few really warm days we get each year, generating crowds at the golf course and sending people to wade in the numerous rivers flowing into the lake, their flows tempering the frigid water.

Mondays and Tuesdays are my days off but somehow my new role as reserve deputy made me feel compelled to return to work. Or, it may have been my preference to seek refuge from the heat in the air conditioning at Whistling Pines. I rushed past the receptionist, Bonny, who sits under an old moose head rescued from one of the downtown bars before the bulldozer took it down. The unnamed moose and knotty pine paneling add to the northwoods feel of Whistling Pines, giving it a feel more like a lodge than a senior citizens residence.

I avoided eye contact with any of the residents, knowing it would lead to a discussion or a question about this week's bingo prizes. I drew a mug of coffee from the dining room urn and took a quick look out of the dining room windows at Lake Superior.

When I walked through my office door Brian Johnson was sitting at my desk flipping through a pile of sheet music. He sensed my entry and spun around in the chair. "I thought I'd give you a day to look over the music for the band-shell park concert and then check in."

"You're lucky I came to work on my day off," I said.

"You're lucky I came over so you didn't have to chase me down."

"Thanks," I said.

"I really came over to see if you're still willing to be the director on Thursday. After the emergency with Sheila, I thought you might want to pass the baton."

"I've been thinking about the peanut in Sheila's reed case."

"I'm afraid you lost me," Brian said.

"Sheila O'Keefe had a severe allergic reaction," I explained. "Someone put a peanut in the pill bottle she was using to keep her reed moist."

Brian smiled. "Everyone knew about her reed cases. She'd pull her reed out of a little brown bottle and noisily suck on it while she assembled her bassoon."

"Oh man," I said. "How did the rest of the band react?"

"It just added to the irritation," Brian replied.

"Did you notice anyone in the band or near the band-stand eating peanuts before the concert or during the intermission?"

Brian thought for a second and said, "Eating peanuts isn't a problem for the stringed instruments or percussionists. They might get greasy fingers but it wouldn't screw up their instruments. None of the brass or woodwinds would eat a peanut during a concert. It would foul their instruments.

"So, you'd be looking at the drummer, the string-bass player, the violinist, and the cello. That narrows the field of suspects a lot. Sheila opened her case backstage and then she ran onto the bandstand, so no one would've had time to put a peanut in her reed case before the concert unless they had access to her instrument case in her car or at her house.

"The emergency room doctor said her reaction came quickly after the exposure, so she wasn't exposed to the peanut until after the intermission," I explained. "Did you notice anyone eating peanuts during the break?" I asked.

"No one offered me a peanut," Brian said, "if that's what you're asking. That's probably the only way I would've noticed someone eating peanuts. Mostly I was talking with you and the trombonists."

"So the trombonists were busy with you, so they're in the clear. I saw you laughing. What was the topic?"

Brian smiled. "What happens in the back row stays in the back row."

"What?"

"It's an old joke. The tubists, trombonists, and euphoniumists sit in the band's back row and don't tell stories on each other."

"I don't think euphoniumist is a word," I said.

Brian smiled, "Actually, it is a word. I've sometimes heard them called euphonists and the British call them euphists."

"Most people call them baritone players," I replied. "Most people couldn't identify a euphonium if you showed them a picture of it."

"Their loss," Brian said as he pressed past me and paused in the doorway. "Do you know how playing a tuba is like having elderly parents?" I shook my head. "They're both unforgiving and hard to get in and out of cars." With that, he was out the door.

"Brian!" I called after him.

"Yes," he said as he stuck his head around the door jamb, with a cherubic smile on his face.

"Do the tuba jokes ever get any better?"

With a dramatic swing of his arm he covered his chest and threw his head back. "Peter," he said with Shakespearean flair. "You cut me to the quick." After a moment he recovered and stood normally. "I only tell you the good ones." He winked. "Is there anything else?"

"Nothing that comes to mind, but it might be nice to have your cell phone number in case something comes up."

He rifled through his wallet and pulled out a business card. It said "Brian Johnson," listed his occupation as "Tubist," and had a cell phone number and an e-mail address.

I read the card and asked, "You're advertising yourself as a tubist. Do you play with other groups besides the Two Harbors band?"

"I pick up gigs every now and then with a small ensemble, playing polka music at wedding receptions, but that's irregular and the accordionist is an octogenarian who sometimes forgets which song we're playing. Other than that, I get an occasional request to sit in with some local groups who are staging musical plays."

"Like the Lester Park Theater?" I asked.

Brian's eyes twinkled as he made the connection. "You're Audrey Rogers' son!"

"Yes, but you don't need to spread that around."

"I'd swear she was a tubist if I didn't know better. She emotes like a melodrama villain and tells jokes like a sailor. She's a hoot at the cast parties."

"Yes, I bet she is."

I thought about Sheila, who was obviously a bit of an irritation to the band. She skipped rehearsals and showed up late for performances. Those things annoy the other band members, but would anyone be angry enough to kill her? I'd screwed up when she walked onto the stage. If I'd been more observant and less shocked by the cocktail dress and her natural beauty, I might've noticed someone who seemed angry when Sheila walked onto the platform.

Maybe it was her appearance. All the other band members were dressed conservatively in white shirts and blouses over black pants, skirts, and slacks. I couldn't even recall any of the women wearing skirts. Sheila was so over the top in her dress that maybe someone snapped.

Brian warned me about Sheila's appetite for younger men. Had she recently dumped a lover? Was she dating a married man? Did an angry wife find out about an affair? Was I imprinting a stereotype on her because of her looks and attire? Was there an ex-husband on the outskirts of the picture?

Another question kept gnawing at the back of my mind, refusing to surface. With a sudden flash of the obvious I grabbed a note pad and scrawled the question that seemed most strange. "Sheila had the 3rd place quilt?" My stereotypical quilter was over fifty, and meticulous, willing to spend endless hours alone picking out, trimming, and pinning pieces of fabric, then carefully sewing them into the intricate patterns that won prizes. Sheila just didn't seem to fit any of those categories but I really didn't know her well although I now suspected she was probably close to that age. She was obviously artistic and right-brain artistic flair often spills into other creative avenues.

Wendy stuck her head in my office, jarring me back from my musings. "Pete, I need a four-letter word for scalawag, and jerk doesn't fit." She tapped a pencil with a gnawed-off eraser and teeth marks on the yellow paint, staring at the crossword puzzle intently.

"Try Roué," I said.

"Spell it," she said, scrubbing the stubby eraser on her previous answer.

"R-O-U-E," I replied. "If you're being proper, there's an accent on the E."

She wrote letters in four boxes then quickly filled in more letters. "Um, thanks," she said, and disappeared. Before I turned around I saw her head was peeking around my doorframe again.

"Would you like to stop off somewhere and get a drink after work?"

"Technically it's my day off, but I'm not opposed to grabbing a beer later. Let me see if Jenny has any plans for us."

"Um, I was thinking that maybe you and I could go alone. You know, to get to know each other outside of work."

"Having been to a few of your band gigs, and seeing too much of the teddy bear tattoo that hides under your turtleneck, I thought we knew each other pretty well." I hesitated and then thought back to the nude women on my computer screen after Wendy's date with another sleaze ball. "Are you talking about going on a date?"

Wendy cocked her head and considered her answer. "I'm not sure. It's just that I've had such a long string of losers, I thought maybe spending an evening with a nerdy guy with no life outside of work might give me an indication about whether I could be satisfied with that kind of relationship."

"I can understand that," I replied. "You can sit around the house eating frozen pizza and drinking beer with Jenny and me."

Wendy cocked her head the other way. "I'd rather give it a try without Jenny around. You know, just in case we really hit it off and want to move along."

"That's not happening," I replied. "You flirted with me when I first started here and you said my life was way too boring."

"Well, maybe I'm at a different point in my life where boring might be more...palatable. You know, maybe it's time for the quiet life of watching television all evening and going to bed after the news, making love to my hubby and then getting a few hours of sleep before work." She paused and asked, "Do you have a tattoo? I think I'd feel more comfortable with someone who has a tattoo. You know, someone who's enough of a bad boy to get a tattoo, but with enough discretion to locate it where it wouldn't show up at work."

"If I think of someone like that I'll let you know. I'm already spoken for."

"Do you have a tattoo?"

"It's irrelevant. I'm in a committed relationship."

"Are you sure? You've been dating Jenny like, forever, and you don't seem to be taking that relationship anywhere. Maybe you need a change of pace. You know, ratchet up the romance side of your life."

"No, Wendy, you're barking up the wrong tree. Go away and work on your crossword."

I looked through the music. A few of the marches were unfamiliar to me, but nothing terribly difficult for a group of experienced musicians. Overall, I was impressed with the band and the director's choice of music. Surprisingly, I had a few butterflies and a little apprehension as I flipped through the songs a second time. I was about to put the music away when I remembered seeing "The Triumphal March" from *Aida.* The second movement had a bassoon solo. Sheila needed to be at the concert.

I fumbled around in the music and found Brian Johnson's cell phone number. He answered on the second ring. "How can I reach Sheila?" I asked.

"With both arms?" he asked.

"No, seriously, I need to talk to Sheila. She has a solo Thursday and I have to know if she's going to show up."

"Would you show up for the next concert if someone had just poisoned you?" he asked.

"I don't know. And that's irrelevant because I need to know if she's going to be at the concert. If she doesn't plan to play, I have to ask John Carr to play the solo with the tenor sax, or I should drop the song from the play list."

"She works at the bank in Silver Bay. I think she's a loan officer or something."

"Thanks," I said, thinking about how long it would take to drive to Silver Bay and back.

"Um, Peter, don't let her get you alone. I saw her looking at you like a side of beef hanging in the butcher shop."

"Really?" I asked, thinking of my discussion with Wendy and starting to feel paranoid about unwanted female attention.

"Well, I did see her looking at you, but it might've been because you were directing the band."

The drive to Silver Bay, the next town closer to Canada, took less time than it took me to find the bank. The low brick building had a flagpole in front and looked amazingly like a library. The bank wasn't large and a few offices lined the north wall. I stood in a teller line until I reached the front and asked for Sheila. The teller asked me to stay at her station while she walked to the corner office. After a short discussion she motioned for me to come over.

A tall, fit, well-groomed man was slipping his suit jacket on as he approached the door. He flashed a smile of bleached teeth and offered his hand. He had a firm grip with a hand that had seen a manicurist more recently than it had seen manual labor. "I understand you're looking for Sheila. If you need a loan, I can offer my assistance." His smile was blinding. "I'm Ron Breck."

"I'm Peter Rogers, the temporary director of the Two Harbors band, and I'd hoped to speak with Sheila about Thursday's concert."

The smile melted and he pointed to a guest chair in front of his cherry desk. As I checked out the certificates of appreciation for support of local charities and ball teams, he slipped his coat off and hung it behind the door. His desk was bare except for a professional photo of him with a beautiful woman and two small girls sitting on the rocky Lake Superior shore.

"Sheila's not here," he said as he sat heavily in his leather chair.

I sat, waiting for more, but that was the full extent of his offering. "Do you expect her later, Ron?" I asked.

"I'm not sure. Probably not."

I was stymied. I had played the card of band conductor and got no response. Did I dare press ahead as the reserve deputy investigating Sheila's attack? I decided to stay low key; besides, I was certain he wasn't going to turn over private information from her personnel file to some guy he's never met with questionable credentials. "Is there some way I can contact her? She has a bassoon solo Thursday night and I need to know if she's well enough to play."

He drummed his fingers on his desk and stared at a spot behind my left ear.

"Sheila had a severe allergic reaction during the concert at the fairgrounds," I said, assuming I was sharing background he already knew. "I'm concerned she not feeling well and she has a solo in the second set of songs. I need to know if she's well enough to play."

"I haven't seen her today," he said, changing his gaze from the corner to my nose. "She called and said she was working from home, but she's logged onto the server. I have no idea where she is or when she'll be back in the office." He continued to drum his fingers on the desk.

"Can you give me her phone number?" I assumed her address would be confidential. "Maybe a bank cell phone number?" I added.

He ran his fingers across his lips in a motion that made me feel like he was telling me, with body language, that his lips were sealed. His eyes darted to a walnut plaque mounted near the corner. "You might try to 'friend' her on Facebook."

His response was so odd I said, "I'm surprised you'd refer me there to contact her."

"I can't give you anything from her personnel file, but I understand she's usually active online."

I looked at the computer on the corner of his desk. "Can you pull up Facebook so we can look at her site?"

"No," he replied.

"Let me guess. Her home page isn't appropriate for the office?"

"Rumor has it, that she has interesting photos, status updates. I've refrained from venturing there, hoping we could maintain a professional work relationship."

"Is she a good employee? I asked.

"Good is a rather subjective word. She writes a lot of loans for us and her customers have financial qualifications that please the bank's investment committee."

"Based on what I've heard, I'm guessing that most of her loan customers are men," I said.

"Yes," he said, almost squirming.

"I'd also guess her work ethic and office apparel are less than totally professional."

"You're Peter Rogers," he said, a look of recognition swept his face. "You're the one who found the bagpipers for Axel Olson's funeral last spring."

It was my time to squirm. "Yes, I was in charge of the arrangements for Axel's funeral."

Ron's smile returned. "I heard that the British honor guard and band were incredible. I'd like to know what strings you pulled to make those arrangements."

"It just fell together," I said, knowing the arrangements had been an accidental convergence of many items far beyond my control.

"People will be talking about that funeral for years. You are legendary."

"Thanks," I said, hoping to close the funeral discussion. "The best place for me to contact Sheila is her Facebook page? Really?"

Ron rose from his chair and closed the office door. "Between you and me," he said, returning to his chair, "I have no idea how to contact her. You can leave a voicemail on her bank phone, but I don't know when she checks the messages. I've heard she's on Facebook regularly. Start there." He rifled through a stack of business cards and handed me one of Sheila's cards. It showed she was a loan officer for the bank and the phone number had a Silver Bay prefix, which made me think it would ring at her desk and not on a cell phone.

"I take it that Sheila isn't employee of the month very often," I said, pocketing the card.

"If she didn't write more high quality loans than all the other loan officers combined, I'd be helping pack up her office. Although I'm not sure we could clear the dust on her desk without a hazmat team."

"If she's not here regularly, where does she find the customers?" I asked.

"I have one loan officer who entertains customers at the golf course through his contacts with the Kiwanis and

Lions Club. The rumor mill says that Sheila spends a lot of time at the gyms in Silver Bay and Two Harbors and leverages those contacts into loan applications. She also has a large sailboat in Duluth and she does a lot of customer entertaining on the water. I have adopted the "Don't ask don't tell" policy when it comes to Sheila."

"I'll leave a voicemail for her, then I'll try Facebook," I said, rising from the chair and shaking his hand.

"Good luck, Peter," he said, shaking my hand again. "If you ever want to talk about a loan or moving your banking here, I'd be happy to work with you."

Since I didn't have a computer to access Facebook at home, I drove back to Whistling Pines and opened Facebook. A quick search pulled up Sheila O'Keefe's home page. Her picture was a glamour shot taken a decade ago and her status was "available." I sent her a "friend request" and as I started to shut down the computer it "pinged" and I was notified that my friend request had been accepted.

I saw the green dot indicating she was actively online so I fired off an instant message and asked, "Will you be at Thursday's concert?"

I waited for a response. "Meet me," popped up.

"Why?" I typed.

"I want to talk, face-to-face."

"I'm busy," I typed.

"Blackwoods in half an hour or I won't show Thursday."

"OK," I replied, again considering Brian Johnson's admonition about not meeting her alone bouncing through my head. *Blackwoods was a public restaurant. There'd be people there. I'd be at a table with her, but there'd be people around,* I kept thinking.

I arrived at the Blackwoods restaurant a few minutes early. The hostess took me past a bank of flaming ovens with chickens slowly roasting on spits and sat me in the dining room. The dark wood and roughhewn timbers made it feel like an upscale north woods lodge, but that was offset by the view of cars passing on Main Street. I declined any beverage, thinking alcohol might lead to an unwanted lowering of inhibitions, and that might prove deadly from a relationship standpoint.

The dining room was filled with business people, dressed in business casual. Khaki pants and golf shirts dominated. Sheila was fashionably late and when she entered, every male head turned. Her blonde hair was tied back in a short ponytail and she was wearing a pink tube top that enhanced her attributes, and white shorts, leaving me with the impression she was trying to look twenty.

I was seated at a table with two chairs on one side and a bench seat on the other. I'd chosen one of the chairs, assuming I might get trapped alongside her if I sat on the bench. Instead of choosing the bench, she took the other chair and pulled it tight against mine, grabbing my arm, rubbing it emphatically.

"It's so cold in here. I'm freezing."

Our waitress was quickly at our table, looking rather haggard from serving the large lunch crowd. "Can I bring you something to drink?" she asked as she set two coasters on the table.

"I'll have an appletini," Sheila said.

"Just water for me," I said.

Sheila gave me a sad look that accentuated the lines around the corners of her mouth and the crow's feet around her eyes. Now I guessed her age to be forty.

"Just water?" Sheila asked. "Wouldn't you rather have a martini or at least a beer?"

"Brian Johnson just dropped off the music for the Thursday concert and I scanned through it. I need a clear head to read through the arrangement more completely this afternoon," I lied. "How are you feeling?"

"A lot better than the last time you saw me. The EMTs said you saved me by giving me the EpiPen. I guess I owe you my life."

"I'm happy it all turned out well," I replied. "Which brings me to the question: Are you planning to play in the park Thursday?" She shivered and quickly looked away, obviously uncomfortable with the question. I quickly added, "You don't need to answer right now, but we'd really like to have you back. I see you have a solo in 'The Triumphal March.'"

The appletini arrived and she drank from it deeply. "I don't know if I'll be up to it," she replied. "The police chief interviewed me. He thinks someone deliberately put a peanut in my reed case. That's a very cruel thing to do."

"Can you think of anyone who might do something like that?"

"Not any of the men," she replied, flashing a coquettish smile and looking better. The alcohol was starting to hit her. "I suppose there are a few women who might be jealous of the attention I get."

"Has anyone ever threatened you?" I asked.

"Not directly," she said, draining her drink and signaling the waitress for another. "Are you sure you don't want something?"

"I don't think so," I replied. "Did you notice anyone tampering with your reeds during the intermission?"

She shook her head and said, "I was feeling a little dehydrated by the heat so I bought a bottle of water." She looked around like she was trying to escape my questions. The waitress arrived with the refill and asked if we'd made our lunch choices. I ordered the planked salmon, thinking the cost was about a half-days pay, and then shuddered at the thought that I might be picking up the costs of the appletinis and Sheila's lunch, too. Sheila ordered a Caesar salad with a grilled chicken breast.

"You're a very talented musician," I said. "The band wouldn't be the same without your bassoon."

She smiled politely and sipped her drink. "I take a lot of pride in my music." She paused and stared out the window for a moment. "I suppose someone might be jealous of my talent."

"Do you think there might be a jealous spouse somewhere out there?"

Sheila shrugged and said, "I seriously doubt that."

"Are there any specific suspects you'd like to share?"

Sheila leaned against me again. "You're dating that skinny nurse. Do you think she's the jealous type?"

"It'll never be an issue," I said firmly.

She first gave me a playful smile. "Oh, are you like Jessie, more into boys than girls? I understand that music attracts some folks with mixed sexuality. Are you into boxers or tighty-whities?"

Lunch arrived and thankfully provided a break in the banter. Sheila ordered another refill.

"You really need something to loosen up. You're wound too tight," she said as she sliced the chicken breast atop her salad. "Someone said you were a Marine in Iraq. Is that true?"

"I was in the Navy," I replied, leaving the details unsaid.

"I've heard sailors always have a hot meal and a dry bed," she said. "It must be awfully lonely sitting on a boat for months at a time. I suppose you really blow off steam when you get into port?"

I was surprised by her question and her ability to slide it into the conversation without missing a beat. I could feel the color rising up my neck. She was reveling in my discomfort.

"Ooh. Did I hit a sore spot?"

"Can we get back to the band?" I asked.

"We can go anywhere you want."

"I'd really like to have you on the bandstand Thursday night." I put my utensils down and pushed my chair away from her to regain some personal space. "Sheila, I think you're a talented musician and an obvious asset to the City Band, but I'm really not interested in anything more personal with you than possibly giving you a hug after your spectacular solo Thursday night. Can you live with that?" Two businessmen at a nearby table overheard the exchange and were apparently amused.

Sheila licked her lips, drained her drink, and straightened up. She signaled the waitress for our bill. "Are you interested in a business or home loan?" she asked.

"I don't think so," I said, confused by the strange question.

When the waitress arrived, Sheila pulled a VISA card from the back pocket of her shorts and put it into the folio, handing it back to the waitress. "We just had a meeting to discuss your possible loan and the business lunch is on my expense account."

"Oh, thank you."

Suddenly sober, she said, "Not a problem. The bank gives me a business account and I use it discreetly. I generate more good business for them than any other loan officer without spending half my afternoons on the golf course or sitting in a bar with my buddies. I spend several hours a day at the gym making contacts, and the bank pays for my membership. No one at the bank complains."

Something gnawing at the back of my brain came to the surface as we waited for the waitress to return. "I saw your quilt at the fair. It was impressive."

The compliment caught her off guard. "Um, thanks."

"How long did it take you to sew the quilt?"

She nervously drank from her already empty martini glass. "It took months."

The waitress arrived with the receipt and she signed quickly without further comment.

"Please come to Thursday's concert," I said, standing as she rose from the table.

She turned and took a step, then looked back at me. Something in her veneer had cracked and her face lost its hardness. "I'll be there Thursday night and I'll be spectacular. Try to keep me alive."

The swing in her hips was gone, replaced by a determined stride as she left the restaurant.

Chapter 18

I spent the rest of Monday afternoon walking the shoreline of Lake Superior near the boat launch. I climbed around the huge black boulders inhaling the scent of the big lake and trying to remember the details of the night the band played at the fair. I was coasting on adrenaline most of the night and really couldn't remember anything related to Sheila or the things going on around her chair on the bandstand.

I'd been nervous about the meeting between my mother and Jenny's parents and I'd looked back at them several times to see if mother had arrived, and then worried about the dinner afterwards and the potential fireworks between Mom and Jenny's parents. My fears were unfounded, mostly because Jenny's parents were very nice, quiet Scandinavians. I could hardly imagine a better outcome for the evening. Well, except for the outing of my military past. Even that turned out better than I could've expected. Now I've earned Jenny's parents' respect, and approval.

I sat on the rocks and stared at the blue swells as they slapped against the rocks. The warm wind was blowing from shore, leaving only the slightest scent of fish and seaweed. Gulls squawked overhead, then swept out toward an incoming fishing boat. The fishermen often cleaned their catch and dropped the offal behind the boat as they approached the harbor. The gulls flew out to meet the boats, hoping for an easy meal.

My thoughts turned to my lunch with Sheila, which was just as tense as the dinner with our parents. Sheila had sexuality that many men found attractive. I found it off-putting.

I walked off the riprap and found some small stones worn smooth by eons of rolling against each other in the waves. I chose a flat stone and skipped it across the water. The gulls were screeching and diving behind the incoming boat. The fishermen call the gulls flying rats and the birds were in a feeding frenzy. I wondered if most men reacted that way to Sheila.

I walked back to my car and sat on the hood. The fishing boat eased up to the quay and tied off. I watched the two men load the boat onto a trailer and pull it up the ramp where they rinsed it down. They laughed and horsed around as they stowed gear and loaded coolers into the back of their Suburban. I needed to go fishing for a day. Fresh air, male bonding, maybe a fish to cook up for supper, all away from Whistling Pines, Sheila O'Keefe, and the attempt on her life. It seemed like such a great escape from reality. Too bad a day-long charter would cost half a month's wages.

I closed my eyes and thought about the concert. I was on the podium and the band was tuning. I was ready to signal the band to raise their instruments when Sheila emerged, stage right, winding her way through the impatient musicians. I remember being shocked by her plunging neckline, the sausage-skin tightness, the sequins, and the amount of thigh showing when she sat in the chair. The bassoon was hanging from her neck and the reed was already in her mouth, clamped between her front teeth. She set three bottles next to her chair, put the reed in the mouthpiece, and tuned. I was so captivated by the scene that I didn't notice the rest of the band reacting to her. It was all about Sheila, just as she wanted it.

Chapter 19

I drove back into town past the golf course/curling club, an unusual combination anywhere but northern Minnesota, and stopped for groceries. My checkbook knew the month-end pinch of finances, but my cupboard said it was time to refill. I walked the aisles, carefully selecting items dictated by coupons and the newspaper ads sitting by the entrance. Hamburger was on sale and versatile. Instant oatmeal was quick and filling. I didn't use milk fast enough to consume a half-gallon before it started evolving into a new life form. Jenny's words about scurvy popped into my head as I walked down the canned vegetable aisle, so I picked up a couple cans of green beans and a can of corn that were three for two bucks. Generic baked beans were inexpensive and filling, sometimes making a meal themselves if Jenny wasn't around. The store brand of bread was on sale, a little doughy, as children prefer, but chock full of calories and with enough chemicals to keep it free of mold for at least a couple weeks. I had a coupon for peanut butter and I splurged on a jar of grape jelly. I checked out and the total left a little black ink in the checkbook, so I declared the trip a success.

I drove back to my house with plans to fry a burger, jam it between a couple slices of bread, and pick up my guitar to try a few new songs I'd chosen for the weekly sing-along at Whistling Pines. There's an old saying about the best laid plans of mice and men, and my plans went out the window when I drove past my neighbor's house.

Dolores was sitting on her porch, making use of her wicker porch furniture. Because of the short Two Harbors summers, called the "poor sledding season" by many of the locals, the wicker spent more time covered in snow than warming in the sun. She waved frantically as I drove past, so I pulled into my driveway and set my groceries on my front step before walking to check on Dolores. I expected to be asked to take another picture of her toe to show the doctor the progression of whatever was happening.

"Peter! I'm so glad you're here!" Dolores pushed herself out of the chair and limped to the top of the steps. Although the temperature was in the 70s she wore a long dress and a gray sweater. She had an amazing amount of energy. I was always concerned that she'd fall and break a hip during one of her daily outings but she was like the mail service: Neither sleet nor snow nor dark of night kept her from her appointed rounds. She had to be at the Catholic Church for Sunday mass and Wednesday bingo. The senior center served broasted chicken for lunch on Tuesdays and she never missed pasty (pronounced like nasty) day on Thursdays. Her Mondays were unstructured and she frequently chose to bake and I was often the beneficiary of her baked goods. Some were edible. Today, it wasn't about her cooking.

"There was a woman here," Dolores said as she limped down from the porch, grasping the railing securely between steps. "She knocked on the door and then walked in the house. I thought she looked suspicious, so I walked over to check her out."

I had a chilling vision of her confronting someone really threatening. I knew from history that Dolores was fearless, but she wasn't invincible. "Was it someone you knew?" I asked.

"No, not at a distance," she said, walking across the uneven grass, using her cane for stability. "She came out when I got to the steps and I recognized her as the bassoon player from the City Band."

"Sheila was here?" I asked, surprised.

"She carried something in," Dolores said, pushing past me. "It was small." She passed the bags of groceries I'd set on my front step and walked into the house. She took a few steps into the house and stopped at the kitchen entrance. "I think it's that flower vase."

On the center of the kitchen table was a crystal vase with a single yellow rose. I opened the card leaning against the vase. The inside was blank except for the words, "Thanks for being there when I needed help."

"Aren't you still going out with that little blonde?" Dolores asked.

"Yes," I replied, not sure what else to say.

"That Sheila, her tight little pink top didn't leave much to imagination. In my day, a woman didn't flaunt her figure like that. I think it's better to leave a little mystery for a man."

I closed the card and folded it in half before tossing it into the kitchen wastebasket. The disposal of the rose was more difficult. It was symbolic of Sheila's misguided attention, so it had to go, but it was pretty. I handed the vase to Dolores.

"A pretty flower for a pretty lady," I said.

She looked at the flower and appeared troubled. "Roses are pretty, but they just don't hold up very well."

"Enjoy it while it lasts."

"Have you tried the piccolo yet?" she asked as she retreated to the front door, the rose in one hand and her cane in the other.

"I've played some, but I've been a little busy with the City Band this week."

"John Phillip Sousa wrote a lovely march that features a piccolo solo. The band always plays it as the finale of the last concert. 'Stars and Stripes Forever' is the song."

"I think it would be a little presumptuous of me to step in as the guest conductor and assign myself a solo. Especially since I've only been playing the piccolo for a week."

Dolores gave me a dismissive wave and walked to the door. "I would personally like to hear you play the piccolo solo in 'Stars and Stripes Forever.'"

"Did you play the piccolo solo with the band?" I asked.

Dolores stopped on my front step and turned. "It was the Fourth of July and VE Day was just behind us. We were all hoping the Japs would surrender before any more boys were killed in the Pacific. I'd been playing flute in the City Band for most of the war, and the director asked me if I'd ever played the piccolo. I said I owned a piccolo, but I hadn't played enough to be proficient. He told me to start practicing because he had a special event coming up. A week before the Fourth he gave me the music for 'Stars and Stripes Forever' and told me I was playing the piccolo solo."

"I'm sure you were fabulous."

"I was scared to death. I practiced day and night, and I fumbled my way through it. At that point in time it didn't matter. The whole country was tired of the war but still full of patriotism. The crowd gave us a standing ovation." She paused at the door and added, "A little girl, named Abby Finch, asked me to come back and play a piccolo duet with her during this week's final concert. When I said no, she said she wasn't playing the Stars and Stripes solo alone. I told her I knew someone who could play it with her. That's you."

I stared speechless at the door after she limped away. After fifteen months in Iraq we'd been moved to Kuwait and from there we flew back to Dover Air Force Base in

Maryland. When I walked down the ramp from the plane the Air Force band was playing "Stars and Stripes Forever." Tears rolled down my cheeks at the thought of that arrival. For a whole year I was sure I'd die in Iraq and the sound of the Air Force band playing Sousa was the first time I really believed I was going to live.

It would be a strain to direct "Stars and Stripes Forever," much less play a piccolo duet. It wasn't happening no matter how much it would disappoint Dolores or Abby Finch. I wasn't about to stand in front of the crowd and break into tears if I had a flashback.

I unloaded the groceries and folded the bags, then went to my bedroom and took out the piccolo. When I blew into it the notes were shrill. After a few abortive attempts I ran through a few scales and managed to crowd my fingers close enough to make clear, distinct notes. I chided myself for not bringing the music home from Whistling Pines, but after digging through a few music books in the piano bench I found a book of marches and opened it to "Stars and Stripes Forever." I played it through once on the piano without falling apart and then attempted the piccolo solo. I bumbled through it a couple times then stumbled through it a couple more times before finally producing something that met my personal expectations.

I was startled by applause at the living room door. I spun and Jenny was standing there with a silly grin, slowly clapping. I felt the color rising in my neck.

"For someone who claims not to have played the piccolo before, that sounded pretty good," she said. "That sounded very familiar. What song is it?"

"Stars and Stripes Forever," I replied as I put the piccolo back into its tiny case.

"Is the band playing that Thursday?" she asked as she walked into the kitchen with a shopping bag slung on her arm. The end of a French baguette extended beyond the top of the bag.

"Apparently it's a tradition to play it as the last song of the year-end concert," I replied. "Dolores asked if I'd played her piccolo yet and told me she wanted me to play it Thursday. I decided to give it a test drive. It went OK, but you don't put someone on stage, playing an unfamiliar instrument, based on one semi-successful attempt."

"You sounded professional. I think you should consider playing it." I heard water running and pans clattered as she set them on the stovetop.

"As guest conductor I can't just step in and assign myself a song." I said, migrating to the kitchen door.

"Why not? Don't you think the band could handle it?"

"It's not my place to step in and play during the second concert I've directed."

Chapter 20

The aroma of Italian tomato sauce filled the kitchen while Jenny dug through my cupboards. "Don't you own a colander?" she asked, stretching to look into the cupboard above the refrigerator. Noodles were boiling on the stove next to bubbling spaghetti sauce.

I reached over her head and pulled the colander from the top shelf of the cupboard. I made a show of blowing the dust from it, which elicited a groan. She took it from me and scrubbed it with soap under hot water.

"I'm surprised you're here," I said as I broke off a piece of the French bread and rubbed it across the stick of butter she'd put on a saucer. "Not that I'm complaining. I like to have you around, but you don't usually show up two nights in a row." *Not even when invited,* I thought.

"It's so weird. Dad and Jeremy are bonding and they told me to find something to do for the night. They caught a steelhead, or something, last night and they're going back to see if they can catch some more." The timer rang and Jenny pulled the boiling noodles off the stove and poured them into the colander. "I don't suppose you have a bottle of Chianti in the wine cellar?"

I have a cellar but I tend to buy wine one bottle at a time and the bottles rarely survive an hour. An obvious solution came to mind.

"I happen to be out of Chianti but I do have a couple bottles of Lake Superior Lager that are at their peak. They are equipped with the latest in sealing technology," I said as I twisted off the caps. "I think Chianti is overrated."

Jenny brought the pot of sauce to the table and set it on a cast iron trivet shaped like a pear. As she went to the sink for the colander of noodles she said, "Red wine has fewer calories than beer." As she set the colander on a plate she added. "I like having dinner with you, but my body isn't accustomed to regular meals with the amount of calories you take in."

"I eat salad...sometimes," I said as I piled pasta onto my plate, "and I have vegetables and fruits regularly...sort of."

"I heard you solved the mystery of Tinker's injury."

"Yeah, I'm a regular Sherlock Holmes. I saw an Amish guy selling rubber-band guns and had a blinding flash of the obvious." I broke off another piece of bread and spread butter on it. "I wandered back to the scene of the crime, lined up the angle of the shot, and snooped around a little bit. First thing you know, I'm in the stall with the best angle for the shot and I find a rubber-band gun hidden away in a jacket pocket."

"So what happened to the shooter?"

"I told his father the story and the last I heard, Dad was putting the fear of God into him. I don't think anything else is required." Somewhere outside I heard the staccato rattle of a woodpecker through the open windows.

"I thought you would report it to the sheriff and the kid would end up in juvenile hall or something," she said. The rattle of the woodpecker got closer. The deep resonant rattle gave me the impression that it was probably a pileated woodpecker, the largest member of the Minnesota woodpecker family.

"Is the woodpecker pecking on your house?"

"He's a big pileated woodpecker and if he were pecking on my siding, the house would be resonating." The words were hardly out of my mouth before we heard the first "BOOM." I flew from the chair and had Jenny around the waist as we fell to the floor.

"What's going on?" Jenny whispered. "Why are we on the floor?"

"Gunshot." I shushed Jenny and we lay on the floor silently. The woodpecker rattle started again, and was followed by a second "BOOM."

I launched myself from the floor and ran for the front door. Jenny yelled after me, "What's going on?"

"Dolores!" I yelled back as I threw the front door open and ran toward my neighbor's house.

The backyard was covered in a rolling white fog. I could smell the sulfur and nitrates from burnt black powder. My first fear at hearing the gunshots was that someone was assaulting Dolores. Once I saw the smoke and smelled the black powder, I knew it was Dolores who was assaulting someone or something.

She had a collection of valuable firearms, locked in a gun cabinet, and I had the key since a springtime incident when she was shooting at a rabbit from her back porch. She'd either found another key or broken the lock, because her back porch was once again the scene of a shooting.

I paused at the corner of the house and peeked around rather than running headlong into another barrage of gunfire. As I peeked around the corner I felt Jenny against my side.

"What's going on?" she asked.

I pulled Jenny with me as we rounded the corner and walked up the steps. High above us the woodpecker started another series of staccato pecking, assaulting a corner of Dolores' cedar siding. Dolores was standing near her back door trying to measure black powder from an antique powder horn into a brass cylinder. Because of her tremors, more powder was spilling onto the floor than was going into the measurer. I feared another shot would turn the porch into a conflagration.

"Peter," Dolores said, "please measure some powder for me."

She seemed totally unsurprised that I'd shown up on her back porch, and she pushed the brass cylinder to me. On a nearby table was a small wooden cask full of lead shot and alongside the cask was a pile of neatly trimmed cotton pads I assumed she planned to use as wadding to seat and hold the shot charge. A tiny metal tin held an array of brass-colored muzzle-loader caps. As unsteady as Dolores was, I found it amazing that she's managed to put two powder and shot charges into the old double-barrel muzzle-loading shotgun that was propped against the railing. I took the powder measurer and powder horn from her and set them on the table.

"What are you shooting at?" I asked.

Dolores looked at me like I was stupid. "That bird," she replied, pointing at the woodpecker who was trying to find a new spot to peck.

"I thought we'd locked up all your guns," Jenny said, nervously eyeing the antique double-barreled shotgun. It had huge old hammers that used a primer cap to ignite the black powder in the barrels. I guessed that it pre-dated the Civil War.

"Oh no, dear," Dolores replied. "The valuable ones are locked up. I've had to keep one around to deal with vermin and such."

"I'll take care of the woodpecker," I said. "It looks like he's found a rotten piece of wood. I can climb up and replace it tomorrow after work." I took her elbow and guided her back into the house. "If that doesn't work, I'll get a rubber snake and hang it from your eaves."

"A rubber snake?" Jenny asked, following us into Dolores's kitchen.

"Birds are afraid of snakes," I said as I steered Dolores toward a chair.

"Really?" Jenny asked.

"Yes. Everywhere except in Ireland where St. Patrick chased all the snakes away."

"Now I know you're pulling my leg," Jenny said, helping Dolores sit down.

"I swear," I said. "The snakes scare the birds away. Now Dolores, are there any more guns around?"

"Oh no," she replied. "It would be unsafe to have them around where someone might stumble across them. All the others are in the case."

"I think it's best if I take the shotgun home and clean it for you. That old black powder is corrosive and I should get the powder residue out before it pits the bore."

"I heard you playing the piccolo duet, Peter," Dolores said in a change of direction that almost left me behind. "It took you a couple of attempts but you had it down the last time."

"I think it is beyond my powers to add myself to the arrangement," I replied, repeating my earlier statement.

Dolores gave me a sour look. "There's a little girl depending on you. Keep that in mind."

"Jenny," I said, trying to move to a new subject, "please take a look at Dolores's toe. The bingo ladies recommended amputation."

Jenny, always the calm and collected nurse, was amazingly unfazed by my "out of the blue" request and quickly set to unlacing Dolores's orthopedic shoe. She examined the toe through the thick support hose Dolores wore, pinching it and bending it, asking Dolores if any of her actions caused pain, and getting positive responses to each inquiry.

"If it's not causing you much pain," Jenny said as she re-laced the shoe, "I think it's bruised and you should leave it alone."

"My foot aches a little less every day," Dolores said, regaining control of the situation. "And those young doctors are just trying to make money by lopping off perfectly good toes."

"Well, it's not perfectly good," Jenny said, "but there really isn't any reason to amputate if it's not infected or gangrenous."

"It's fine!" Dolores said, rising from her chair and taking a few unsteady steps. "See, I hardly limp at all!"

Back in my kitchen, Jenny re-warmed our plates in the microwave while I stashed the shotgun in the basement with Dolores's .22 rifle, confiscated during the attempted bunny shooting incident the previous spring. I sat down and took a deep breath before realizing that Jenny was staring at me.

"What?" I asked, chewing a mouthful of spaghetti and sauce.

"I have bruises," she replied.

"Huh?"

"I'm bruised from being thrown to the floor. Couldn't you just say, 'Jenny, I think Dolores is shooting a gun? Let's walk to her house and see what's happening?'"

I tipped my head back and took a deep breath. "That would be a rational response. I'm still conditioned from Iraq where a second of delay can mean the difference between being dead or alive. When I hear gunfire I hit the floor and think about it after I'm down."

"You thought about it long enough to throw me down with you."

"I'm sorry, but that's how we made sure the new guys lived long enough to develop their instinctive reaction to gunfire," I replied. "You tackle them as you duck for cover. Most of them catch on pretty quickly. How bad are your bruises?"

She lifted her sleeve and I could see where my fingers had dug into her upper arm when I pulled her off the chair. "I'm sure my hip and left cheek will be colorful tomorrow. You better hope I don't have to go to the doctor for a checkup. They'll have Social Services knocking on your door before nightfall."

"I'm sorry. It's just..."

Jenny got up from her chair and pulled my head to her breast. "I know. It's just instinct." She stroked my hair and I wrapped my arms around her waist. "I just wish your instincts were a little less...physical."

She kissed the top of my head and picked up her plate. "I've lost my appetite," she said before pulling out the wastebasket and scraping the remnants of her spaghetti into the trash. Before putting the wastebasket away, she reached into it and pulled out a white card with spaghetti stains.

"Peter, what's this thank you note in your garbage?"

"It's from Sheila O'Keefe. I tried to talk to Sheila O'Keefe about the night she had the allergic reaction and she dropped off a thank you note and a flower which I gave to Dolores."

"You talked to her here?" Jenny asked, tapping the card on the edge of the sink.

"No, we had lunch at Blackwoods."

"She gave you a card at lunch and you brought it home?"

"No, we had lunch and she stopped by later," I said, suddenly aware of the line of questioning and how it might look like Sheila had stopped off for an afternoon delight. "I was grocery shopping. Dolores saw her walk into the house and came over to investigate."

"Why was she here after lunch? Did she have something to add to her previous testimony?" Jenny's voice was getting sharper with every sentence.

"It wasn't testimony," I replied. "I just asked her if anyone had reason to harm her. We talked about it over lunch."

"Why did she come to your house after lunch?"

"She dropped off a flower and that note," I repeated. "I threw the note away and gave the flower to Dolores. I have no interest in Sheila or her flowers. If I'd been home, I would've refused the flower and told her to leave."

"I've heard rumors about Sheila's business lunches," Jenny said, throwing the card back into the garbage. "The rumor is that she's usually the dessert."

I got up and hugged Jenny. "I have no interest in Sheila other than a professional interest in her musical skills. She's the best and only bassoonist in Two Harbors and possibly the most talented musician in the band." I felt Jenny's muscles relax under my hug.

"Be careful. Sheila's a cougar and loves to chase down good looking younger men, like you. After all her years of conquests, I hate to think about what you might catch from her."

"I'm sure there's nothing a good dose of penicillin wouldn't cure."

Jenny pushed back and looked me in the eye. "I think amputation would be the cure I'd be most likely to apply."

"Ouch!"

"You'd better believe it would hurt. I wouldn't use anesthesia or sharp utensils for the operation." Jenny's blue eyes became suddenly steely.

I remembered her comments about the Norwegian pilot who'd fathered Jeremy. She'd talked about him one night after a few beers and, although she hadn't spilled any tears at the time, it was obvious the topic was terribly painful. I pulled her close, now more attuned to the deep pain she'd felt over the lies and deceit she'd suffered with the breakup of that relationship. That pain wasn't far under the surface.

"You're just as reflexive as I am," I said. "I jump at the sound of bullets and you recoil at the scent of another woman. Do you have nightmares too?"

"Not nightmares as much as fits of crying," she said, letting out a deep sigh. "You can be free if you want to move on. Please just be upfront about it and don't go sneaking around behind my back, hoping I won't notice."

I clenched her tight and I felt her tears soaking through my shirt. I'd done nothing wrong, but I still felt like a jerk for even having lunch with Sheila. "I'm not going anywhere."

Chapter 21

Tuesday

I woke again with tingling in my arm. When I opened my eye I saw Jenny lying in the crook of my elbow, breathing softly. I tried to slip my arm from under her neck without waking her, but as my arm started to slide she murmured and grabbed my wrist.

"I've got to pee," I whispered in her ear. She released my wrist and I slipped out of bed.

The clock said it was a little after five and I could hear the chirping birds outside the open window. As I walked to the bathroom I heard the rattle of the woodpecker on Dolores's siding. I made a mental note to check out the selection of rubber snakes in town. I had a sudden revelation that I couldn't remember seeing a rubber snake in any of the stores. Maybe I'd need to check the Internet.

I spread shaving gel on my face and ran hot water over the razor. I looked at the once young face that stared back at me from the mirror as I scraped the whiskers off. When I'd gone into the Navy I'd looked like a twelve-year-old. Between the horrors I'd seen and the alcohol I'd abused, my boyish looks had changed. My mother said I finally looked like an adult. I'd lost my innocence in Iraq in many ways.

When I got out of the shower Jenny was making a pot of coffee. Her porcelain skin was especially translucent in the early morning light and the thin T-shirt she wore was backlit by the windows and silhouetted her slim figure. The bruises on her arm and hip were highlighted.

"What are you staring at?" she asked as she handed me coffee in a cup with a logo from a farm supply store that went out of business shortly after the Shopko opened.

"I'm just admiring your personal assets."

"I'd think that you'd seen enough of them last night to last you for at least a day," she replied as she poured herself coffee in a cup with a yellow smiley face, the mate to the one I kept in my office.

"You think like a girl, not a guy."

She leaned against the counter and blew on the steaming coffee. "What are your plans for today?"

"I thought I'd try to find a rubber snake."

She shuddered, the goosebumps rising on her arms. "I'd forgotten about the woodpecker problem. Where are you going to find a rubber snake?"

"I suppose my best bet would be a novelty shop."

"Wow, what a brilliant idea. I saw five of those downtown last week," she said with a smirk.

"I thought an Internet search might point me somewhere. In the meanwhile Shopko might be worth a look." I put two slices of bread into the toaster and then savored the aroma of the freshly opened peanut butter, which I thought was second only to the aroma of a fresh can of coffee. When I set the jar on the table I saw Jenny staring at me with a strange look on her face. "What?" I asked.

"I'm not sure you love me as much as you do that jar of peanut butter. You should've seen the expression on your face when you sniffed it."

"You and peanut butter are in separate categories. I love both of you, but in different ways."

"Do me a favor. If Sheila invites you to lunch, please decline the invitation."

A smart-ass retort died on my lips when I looked at Jenny's face and saw how serious she was. "Agreed."

I wandered the Shopko aisles in search of the rubber snake and came up empty. The greeter was genuinely sorry. In fact, she was so sorry that she pulled out her cell phone and called her hairdresser, who polled the ladies in the shop, and told me to try the Sawtooth Mountain Trading Post. At the Trading Post a perky strawberry-blonde clerk with "CLARE" embossed on her nametag, smiled and listened politely when I explained the whole story about the woodpecker and the need to humanely scare it away. Once she was sure I was through with the story she led me to an aisle with a few toys and showed me a rubber snake in the back of a bin. It bore no resemblance to anything indigenous to the region, but woodpeckers are migratory and I hoped he might not be too discerning.

"I think it's been here since I started," she said, handing it to me.

I looked at the green sponge rubber with painted brown strips. "I don't suppose you'll re-order these?" I asked.

Clare smiled and led me to the front counter. "I'll tell you what. If it actually keeps the woodpecker away, you let me know and I'll order some and advertise them as woodpecker repellents." She rang it up and I paid the entire 87 cents, including tax, with change from my pocket.

Dolores watched me pull a ladder out of her garage and insisted she hold it with one hand, her cane in the other, as I climbed to the peak where I installed the snake with a cordless drill and a screw. When I climbed down Dolores looked distressed.

"What's wrong?" I asked as I folded the ladder.

"I'm not convinced the snake will scare the woodpecker away. If this doesn't work, will you shoot the bird?"

I hesitated, considering the potential conversation we'd have if I tried to explain the federal Migratory Birds Act and the illegality of shooting songbirds, including woodpeckers. Instead I just replied, "Sure."

"After you put the ladder away," Dolores said, "wash your hands and I'll feed you lunch. I made a tuna salad."

I balked, but before I had time to decline Dolores was back to her porch, marching toward her kitchen. I returned the ladder to her garage and hung it from dusty hooks on the wall. I looked around and noted that everything was neatly arranged, from wrenches hanging in order of size on a pegboard, to wood boxes carefully labeled, in neat block letters that identified the power tool they contained. Everything had a patina of dust that probably dated back to the death of Dolores's husband. I opened a box marked, "electric drill" and saw a shiny metal drill with the electric cord carefully wound around the drill body and held in place by a cracked red rubber-band. I touched the rubber-band and it disintegrated, as did a portion of the insulation on the electrical cord, exposing the copper wire. I replaced the cover on the box, wondering if I should mention the deterioration of the tools to Dolores, then thought it better that she assumed her husband's workshop was in the same pristine condition he'd left it in several decades ago.

I returned to my house and washed my hands in my own bathroom sink. I changed into a clean T-shirt and was knocking on Dolores's back door within fifteen minutes.

Lunch was carefully laid on the table when I entered the dining room. At a table that would seat a dozen, she'd set two places with flowered china plates, sterling silverware, linen napkins rolled inside silver napkin rings, and iced tea in crystal goblets. On each plate was a cabbage leaf topped with a scoop of tuna salad. The centerpiece was a dainty cut-glass vase with the rose I'd given her flanked on one side by a silver sugar and creamer set and on the other by china salt and pepper shakers that matched the place settings.

I carefully held the chair for Dolores. After she was seated I took my place, slid off the napkin ring, and shook open the napkin. I felt terribly underdressed in my gray Minnesota Twins T-shirt and blue jeans.

"Peter, I'm very pleased you came for lunch. I rarely get to entertain these days."

I looked at the tiny scoop of salad on my plate and quickly considered what I'd eat to finish filling my stomach when I returned to my house. I picked up the iced tea and took a sip, then started coughing.

"Oh dear," Dolores said, starting to rise from her chair.

I waved to keep her seated and covered my mouth with the napkin as I caught my breath. I was unprepared for the liquor on the rocks in my goblet.

"I suppose I should've warned you," she said. "But I saw the bottle of Jack Daniel's by your counter and I thought you'd enjoy a shot of booze."

"I do enjoy it," I replied. "It looked like iced tea and it caught me by surprise." I took another sip to demonstrate my acceptance.

"Joe and I never drank much other than sherry, but he kept a bottle or two around for entertaining. The bottle is on the sideboard. I think it's something French. It's been open a long time. I hope it hasn't gone bad."

The label was French and from what I could tell it was very old Cognac. Although it was smooth, I felt it was being wasted on me. I sampled the tuna, expecting the usual Minnesota recipe with canned tuna, mayonnaise, and maybe a touch of onion and celery. The tuna was suspiciously mild. I quickly realized that Dolores had switched sweetened sour cream for the mayo. There was a crunch, but it wasn't onion or celery. Once again, Dolores had either misread the recipe or had played fast and loose with the substitution of ingredients.

"Your tuna salad is an unusual recipe. I usually make it with mayonnaise or Spin Blend. I've never had one made with sweetened sour cream before," I said.

"Oh dear, I hope you don't mind. The salad dressing was separated so I opened some cream cheese, but it was too thick. I had to thin it with evaporated milk." She hesitated and added, "Did I tell you it was tuna salad? I didn't have any tuna so I used a can of chicken."

I took another bite and I could taste the caramelized evaporated milk. "What are the crunchy bits?" I asked.

"I found a can of water chestnuts in the back of the cupboard," she replied, setting my mind somewhat at ease. "It was behind a can of mandarin oranges that had leaked. I had to pry it loose with a screwdriver."

Uh oh, I thought. If the water chestnuts were behind the mandarin oranges, they were probably older, and the oranges were old enough to eat through the can with the syrup gluing the can to the shelf. I took a healthy swallow of my cognac, hoping it would counteract the metals that had leached out of the cans and into the food. I probably wouldn't need my multi-vitamin with minerals. I put another bite of salad on the fork, relieved that the portion she'd served me was small.

"The woman who brought the rose," Dolores said between bites, "I remember her because she's always dressed like a tramp. You shouldn't have anything to do with her. She has a reputation."

I smiled at Dolores's polite choice of words. "What type of reputation does she have?" I asked, playing dumb.

"She has the kind of reputation that keeps her from getting invitations to the homes of nice people," Dolores said, with obvious discomfort.

"It appears she has plenty of social engagements," I replied.

"Peter, you're missing my point. That woman is a social pariah. It would serve you well to not see her socially. Your blonde friend, Jenny, is very nice, although she has a bit of a reputation herself." Dolores paused and let out a sigh. "I suppose it's more acceptable to have a child out of wedlock these days."

I nodded but said nothing.

"That bassoon player, she was the one who was poisoned at the county fair. I heard that someone put poison elderberry wine in those little pill bottles that she drinks out of during the concerts." Dolores paused, then added, "You probably don't know this, but there are two types of elderberries that look very much alike: One is edible and the other is poisonous. Most people can't tell the difference so they avoid them entirely. The Boyle family could tell the difference and would pick berries and make wine that they gave away to their friends. You never wanted to be one of their enemies because it was said that they also made wine from the poison berries too."

"I don't think anyone named Boyle is in the band," I said between tiny bites of salad.

"It doesn't matter anymore. The Boyles had a big Catholic family and they've all intermarried with other families so it's not safe to drink elderberry wine that anyone gives you anymore. You just have to assume you're getting it from one of the Boyle descendents and you'd better hope they like you. It's not like the Currans. They were Protestants and only had ABC sex, so they hardly had any children or grandchildren."

"Um, I'm not familiar with ABC sex," I said, taking a sip of Cognac and having a hard time believing I was having this conversation with my elderly neighbor.

Dolores looked surprised. "Everyone knows what ABC sex is: Anniversaries, birthdays, and Christmas. Women hardly ever got pregnant on that regimen, although that seemed to be a pretty regular schedule for some couples, especially shy Protestants in the days before the pill."

"Why would that be more of an issue for shy Protestants?"

"Well, if you didn't want to get your wife pregnant, you had to buy condoms at the local pharmacy. If you were shy, you couldn't buy them in town, so you had to go all the way to Duluth or Silver Bay to buy them from a druggist who didn't know you. Unless you had a few spare dollars to stock up on a few of them, you didn't have sex very often."

I couldn't hold my laughter anymore and I snorted a swallow of cognac up my nose. The cognac burned and my eyes watered. Dolores cracked a smile that highlighted the crow's feet at the corners of her eyes and gave me a glimpse of the beauty she'd once been.

"I suppose it sounds funny now, but times were different when you were in polite society," she explained. "The miners moved to the Iron Range towns in droves, most leaving their wives and children behind in their home country. They brought them over after they'd earned enough to buy a house or a couple of acres. If you drive through Biwabik and those old mining towns, on every corner you'll see a building that was once a bar with an upstairs apartment rented out by the half hour. There were a lot of lonely men roaming those streets and a nice girl wasn't seen outside her house after dark.

Dolores looked at the rose and then back at me. "If we were back in the old mining days, I suspect Sheila would be entertaining men in the apartment over one of those old bars. Times have changed and the business has changed, but I think Sheila's making a living bouncing her bottom on a mattress. There are a lot of women in this town who hear the same gossip that I hear, and some of them aren't too pleased about the loans their husbands got from Sheila."

"I think there's a lot of gossip flying around the hair salon and not all of it is true," I said, picking at my salad.

"That's the wonder of gossip, Peter. It doesn't have to be true for people to believe it and some of the people who believe it are Boyle descendents or other folks who know how to use a gun."

Dolores suddenly had my full attention. "Are you hearing threats against Sheila?"

"I'm just saying, if I were you I wouldn't stand in front of Sheila during the concert."

"Who's telling you this?"

"I'm not sure I exactly recall that I heard anyone make a specific threat, but the ladies at bingo all seem to agree that if Sheila shows up none of the musicians will be sitting anywhere near her at the concert."

Dolores slid her chair back and rocked her body a couple times before gaining enough momentum to push herself to a stooped standing position. I jumped from my chair and went to assist her but she waved me away.

"All this talk about Sheila seems to have cost you your appetite," she said, looking at the half scoop of faux tuna salad on my plate. She gathered her plate and utensils before allowing me to finish clearing the table and carry the plates to the kitchen. "You're doing a pretty respectable rendition of the "Stars and Stripes Forever" piccolo duet."

"I gave it a few tries and there are still a lot of squeaks and squawks that don't belong there."

"You'll do well at the concert."

As I scraped the plates into her garbage disposal I again explained I wasn't going to add any part to myself in the concert.

"Like I said, I think it's hardly fair for me to step in and play the piccolo in my second concert with the band."

Dolores was tapping her cane on the floor and it caught my attention. Her eyes were narrow and her lips were tight. "As you recall, Abigail Finch knocked on my door last week. Do you know who she is?" she asked in a stern voice I'd never heard before.

"I don't think we've met," I said.

"Abby is in the seventh grade and she plays flute and piccolo in the school band. She also plays in the City Band"

I ran the mass of faces I'd met at the county fair through my mind. I suddenly remembered a diminutive girl with mousy brown hair and a face speckled with acne. She had been tucked in among the flutists as if they were protecting her. "I remember her now."

She paused for a second. "I told her a piccolo player lived next door and I promised her you'd be playing alongside her. That's why I gave you the piccolo."

"But you didn't know I'd even played a flute before," I protested.

"You can play any instrument you touch. I'll be in the audience and I expect you to play the duet flawlessly. Don't let me or that little girl down." With that, she turned and left me standing in the kitchen holding a china plate dripping chicken salad into the sink.

When I got home I took a deep breath and started looking for the piccolo case. It was tiny and easy to misplace. Once I found it, I played the "Stars and Stripes Forever" piccolo solo until my fingers cramped.

Hours later I heard Jenny open the door just as I played the trill that ends the solo.

"You'll never guess what Dolores did to me," I said as I gently set the piccolo on the piano.

"You said you were going to find a rubber snake and hang it from her eaves."

"That's nothing compared to her other project." My resolve weakened by the Cognac during lunch, I walked into the kitchen and took down two jelly jars that served as my juice glasses. I poured two fingers of Jack Daniels into each and handed one to Jenny.

"I don't like whiskey very much," she said, sniffing the glass tentatively.

"That's OK. Just hold it for me until I finish this one." I threw back the entire shot and set the glass on the worn Formica table top. When I reached for the other glass Jenny pulled it back.

"Not so fast. Will I need this after you tell me about Dolores's mission?"

I eyed the glass, trying to gather polite words while holding back my frustration. "There's a seventh grader in the City Band who plays piccolo. She asked Dolores to come back and play the 'Stars and Stripes Forever' piccolo solo with her because she's too shy to play it alone. Dolores explained that hands were too crippled. Abby said she wouldn't play alone, so Dolores told her I would play the solo with her."

Jenny continued to hold the whiskey out of my reach. "So let me get this straight: Dolores volunteered you to play the piccolo solo with Abby Finch?"

"You know Abby Finch?"

"Sure. She lives down the street and Jeremy has a crush on her, although I'm not supposed to know that. How long have you been playing piccolo?" Jenny asked.

"Two days, three if you count today."

Jenny took a long swig of the Jack Daniels and started to cough. “Wow! That is strong.”

“Why’d you drink it?” I asked.

“*You* have to be sober to practice.”

Chapter 22

Wednesday

Len was smoking his pipe under the portico when I arrived at work. As I approached he tapped the embers out of the pipe bowl into the ashtray on top of the wastebasket. He looked up as I stepped onto the sidewalk and shook his head.

"Looks like you had a couple rounds of Jack Daniels last night."

I waved him into the entryway and we walked through the atrium into the dining room. I drew two cups of coffee from the urn and we sat at a table near the kitchen amidst the clatter of cooking noises mingled with laughter and chatter. The dining room was empty except for Barbie who was arranging place settings and flowers on the tables near the windows.

"Do you know any more about what happened to Sheila?" Len asked.

"I know she's taking the brunt of the local gossip mill and it sounds like every woman in town suspects she's bedding their husbands to prop up her loan portfolio at the bank. I had lunch with her and I think she spends a lot of time working out and meeting people at the gym who later turn into business for the bank." I took a sip of coffee and asked, "How about you?"

"I get the vibe that she dresses rather flashily," Len replied. "All the men think she's hot and all the women think she's a whore. I think she's like one of the Hollywood starlets who's trying very hard to retain her face and figure so she looks like she used to."

"My neighbor Dolores invited me over for lunch," I said. "She made some interesting comments about women poisoning people and men mad enough to use guns."

"Guns? I don't like the sound of that."

"Who's got guns," a voice asked behind me. I turned and Angie Lafond, the head cook, was checking the coffee in the urn. Angie was pretty, in a Goth sort of way with her jet black hair, tattoos, and piercings.

"I think everyone in the county has a hunting gun of some kind," Len answered casually.

"The police chief and Whistling Pines head investigator don't talk about hunting guns over coffee," Angie said. "I'm guessing someone either got shot or is going to get shot."

The kitchen door marked "Exit" swung open and Miriam pushed through with a platter of frosted cinnamon rolls. Their aroma filled the space as did Miriam's personality. "We made a batch of irregular pieces we won't feed to the residents. Help yourselves while they're warm," she said, offering the tray to us.

"Peter and the cop were just talking about people with guns," Angie said to Miriam.

"I've got a shotgun in the barn," Miriam offered. "We have raccoons or skunks that show up in the barnyard now and again."

"No," Barbie wandered over and joined the conversation. "They're talking about a gun to shoot somebody. I'm personally very much against guns and I think the chief should confiscate the guns from anyone he suspects is going to shoot someone."

Len was handling the whole discussion in stride and smiling. I was feeling the aftereffects of the cognac, Jack Daniels, and a short night of sleep due to too much piccolo practice.

Brian Johnson walked in and handed me sheet music. "Do you know how much beer a tuba holds?"

I shook my head.

"Eight and a half gallons plus what's in the tuba player," he said with a smile. He then pointed to the music in my hand. "I know you have the conductor's layout of 'Stars and Stripes Forever,' but after I heard you were doing a piccolo duet with Abby Finch, I thought you might want to have the piccolo part separately."

"Who would put beer into a tuba?" Angie asked.

"Sometimes I just get curious when I'm drinking," Brian replied.

"No one can drink eight and a half gallons of beer," Angie said.

"Who drinks alone?" Brian asked with a shrug.

"You can play piccolo?" Miriam asked me.

"It's an amazing coincidence," replied Brian. "Abby Finch was the only piccolo player and she's only a seventh grader and so shy she wouldn't play the solo unless we found another piccolo player. Luckily, she found out that Peter can play piccolo too."

Miriam read right through me and shook her head. "My, oh my, he's such a talented boy. He plays guitar and piano around here and he's kept the piccolo in hiding. How long have you played piccolo, Peter?"

"I've played flute for years and picking up the piccolo was easy," I lied.

Wendy appeared with her crossword puzzle and a pencil. "Peter's playing piccolo? Well, that explains a lot."

Everyone was suddenly silent as they turned to her. "Like what?" Len asked.

"It looks like he's got a piccolo in his pocket every time he sees Jenny." Everyone groaned and I could feel the red creeping up my neck. She wandered off to a corner table and started penciling answers into the puzzle.

"Did you know that a pinhole can ruin a trumpet, but a tuba can play on with a bullet hole in it?" Brian asked.

"What's the punchline?" Angie asked.

"There's no punch line; it's just an observation. You guys were talking about guns and people being shot, and I thought that was an interesting piece of trivia. If you don't appreciate my trivia, I'll leave. See you at the concert tomorrow, Peter."

"Hey!" Wendy yelled from the back corner of the room. "Who's going to get shot? I might come to the band concert if someone's going to be shot."

"No one's getting shot," Len said emphatically. "But it might be a crime to let these cinnamon rolls get cold without eating one."

That ended the discussion and everyone returned to their jobs.

Len wiped frosting from his lip and leaned forward as the first residents started to filter in for breakfast. "Do you think there's a wife out there mad enough to try to kill Sheila?" he asked.

"I don't think so, Len. Sheila doesn't seem interested in a long-term relationship with anyone, so it's not like she's stealing any husbands. Besides, getting a divorce is easy these days. If a wife can prove that her husband has been cheating on her, I'd bet she would come out on top morally and financially.

"What other motives have you heard about?" Len asked.

"Nothing worth killing someone over unless they're really psychotic," I replied.

"Give me some examples."

"Sheila's chronically late for concerts and skips rehearsals. She dresses provocatively and flirts with the guys. I don't know, maybe it's because she doesn't show up until everyone is already tuned and the whole band has to wait for her. It's got to be something really stupid or invisible."

Chronically confused Hulda Packer, flamboyantly wearing a dress with plumeria flowers printed over it, heard part of the conversation and wheeled over. "Sheila plagiarizes." With that, she was gone.

Len looked confused. "Plagiarizes?"

"Hulda often can't come up with the right word. If you recall, she was the woman who told us that Axel had been killed because he was a philatelist when she meant philanderer."

"So, what do you think she meant when she said that Sheila plagiarizes?" Len asked.

"I can't even think of a word that sounds like plagiarize."

From the back corner Wendy chimed in, "I need a ten-letter word that ends in E-N-T that means go around."

"Circumvent," I replied.

"Does she do that often?" Len asked.

"Anytime she's working on a crossword and I'm within earshot," I replied.

"How often do you know the correct word?"

I shrugged. "Most of the time."

"Why do you know all those answers?"

"Stupid stuff gets stuck in my head and I can pull it out," I said.

"How about pulling out a stupid motive for murdering Sheila?"

"Plagiarizing is about as stupid a motive as I can furnish."

Len rose from the table and reached for his pipe. "I've got to ponder plagiarizing for a while."

Chapter 23

Things more pressing than Sheila's safety were calling me. I didn't have bingo set up. The natives would be restless. It was time to get back to work.

The computer monitor was the centerpiece of my office a pylon of clarity amidst the piles of papers. Although the office gave the appearance of chaos, I knew where each piece of paper was buried in each pile. On the other hand, the computer was a tool that served me well most days and drove me crazy on others. I shut it down at the end of each day and fired it up each morning.

I was concerned when I could hear "Stars and Stripes Forever" playing as I approached my office. When I opened the door I was staring at a Marine Corps band (there are several) displayed on my computer monitor.

As the song hit the two-minute mark three Marines, in dress blues, came forward crisply with piccolos for their solo. As they began to play, my face suddenly appeared on each of their bodies. I recognized my picture from the Whistling Pines web site. Someone managed to Photoshop it into the video.

"Wendy!" I yelled, seeking out the most likely culprit. She caused and solved most of the computer problems, having the most expertise in the facility. She also, like an arsonist, wanted to be around to see the fire.

"What? she replied, magically appearing at my door.

"Make the Marines go away."

"They're playing the national march of the United States."

"I know. Make them go away." By this time the opening bars of the song were re-starting in a new loop.

She sat in my chair, her fingers flying over the keys. "You didn't like the bulls either," she said as the screen went blank and then returned to the randomly twisting loops provided by the manufacturer as the default screen saver. "I thought you'd like to see what the big piccolo show was going to look like with you on the stage."

"How did you do that? You were in the dining room the whole time we were talking about the piccolo plans. How did you beat me back here and put the Marines on the screen?"

Ignoring my question, she got up from the desk chair and said, "Mike Mower wrote a really cool sonata for piccolo and piano. Maybe we can play that for music hour next week."

I plopped into my desk chair and spun to face her. "My piccoloist days are over once Thursday's concert is over."

"Jenny says you're good. You should stay with it."

"No. I turn in my piccolo license Friday."

"You can't," Wendy said with a devilish smile. "You're on the City Band roster now. Membership is perpetual, and if the need comes up for a director or piccolo, you'll get the call."

"What?"

"You're now a life member. Would you like to add any other instruments to your resume? I know that you play guitar and electric bass. There's not much call for them in the band, but I suspect that you also play some brass instruments."

"No."

Wendy shrugged and walked away. I quickly immersed myself in the minutiae of my job. Sheila's plagiarism never crossed my mind.

I felt tired and realized that the early morning caffeine was out of my system. The computer clock said it was nearly ten when I wandered back to the dining room for another cup of coffee. The morning breakfast rush had cleared and Barbie was resetting the tables for lunch. At a corner table overlooking the lawn sat one of the newest residents with "Scooter" Arneson.

Any assisted-living facility has turnover: People leave for more acute care, like a nursing home, or move closer to their children or family. Some die. It's a never-ending cycle that throws new personalities into the mix on a monthly basis. Just on the basis of longevity, the majority of the residents are always women, and it's somewhat of a novelty when a new male resident arrives.

After the unfortunate death of Axel Olsen a few months earlier, and the resulting relocation of "Snuffy" Sarinen, who killed Axel, we got a new male resident, Clarence "Speedy" Putnam. All the old-timers had nick-names, and "Speedy" had been the shortstop for the high school and Two Harbors' baseball teams in the late '40s. Local lore said he still held the school record for the 100-yard high hurdles and stolen bases, although it was hard to visualize the now starkly slender man as a star athlete.

Speedy was having a discussion with Scooter, who was known, in his day, as a speed-demon hotrod driver who could drive and repair anything mechanical. Now he roamed the hallways driving a red Victor motorized scooter with yellow flames painted on the sides. His scooter was parked beside the table where he was making an emphatic statement to Speedy. It sounded like I was just catching the end of a long negotiation.

"But Speedy, the boat would be perfect. It's a Lund 14-footer and the Johnson outboard motor purrs like the day it was built."

"I need a boat like I need a spare set of dance shoes," Speedy replied.

"It'll make us even for that Ford pickup you sold me with the blown engine."

"You knew the engine was blown and you told me you had a spare," Speedy replied. "Besides, I practically gave you that pickup. You only paid me fifty bucks for it."

"Well, this Johnson really pushes that boat along," Scooter said. "It's a thing of beauty and it's just collecting dust in my neighbor's garage."

"I don't need a boat. The kids sold all my fishing gear in a garage sale when I moved here, and it's not my problem that your old neighbor wants you to get the boat out of her garage."

"You've got a grandson who probably fishes a lot. Maybe you could buy the boat for him," Scooter suggested.

Speedy just shook his head. "I'm not that generous."

I brought my coffee to the table and sat in an empty chair. "Good morning, guys." Scooter leaned back, giving me a look that said he was unhappy to have the negotiation interrupted. Speedy smiled and looked relieved.

"What's new in the outside world?" Speedy asked.

"Well, the county fair is over and the city is going back to normal," I replied. "We've got a load of folks taking the van down to the bandshell Thursday night for the last concert of the season."

I could see Scooter staring into space, trying to remember something. Then he said, "I heard the conductor broke a leg and you were taking over. Funny that they always tell actors to break a leg, and here the conductor actually did!"

"What happened to Sheila O'Keefe?" Speedy asked. "I heard she got food poisoning and almost died from eating a bad hot dog at the fair."

"She had a bad reaction to a peanut," I explained. "Someone knew that she's allergic to them and put one into the bottle where she keeps the reeds for her bassoon."

"Huh," Speedy replied. "She's a fine looking woman. I would've taken her out for a cup of coffee and a slice of pie in my younger days."

Scooter was shaking his head. "Candy is dandy, but liquor is quicker," he quoted. His reputation as a heavy drinker was well known and he'd lost his driving privileges several times after being arrested for drunken driving. It was also rumored that he'd been a bit of a ladies man and hadn't been choosey about the marital status of his partners.

Howard Johnson walked to the table and sat in the fourth chair. Howard's dress slacks were freshly pressed, unlike Scooter's blue "Dickies" work pants and Twins t-shirt, or Speedy's jeans and plaid flannel shirt.

"Sheila has a bit of a reputation around town," Howard offered. "I suppose some jealous wife tried to send her a message."

"Hulda Packer said she had plagiarized something and that was why she was targeted," I said.

All three gave me questioning looks, but Speedy said, "Hulda's about as loony as a robin that's been eating fermented mountain ash berries."

"Fermented berries?" I asked.

"The robins fly into windows and trees when they'dve eaten mountain ash berries after the first frost," Speedy explained. "The berries crack when they freeze and then yeast gets inside the fruit and ferments the sugar. The birds get drunk eating them."

"She gets her words twisted," Howard replied, "but she often knows what's going on. She thinks Sheila did something at the fair, causing the attempt on her life."

"She showed up late for the concert," I noted, "so all the other musicians had to wait while she assembled and tuned her bassoon."

"It's something to do with her round heels," Scooter said.

"What are round heels?" I asked.

"If a woman was easy to get into the *missionary position,* people said she had round heels," Howard said with a hint of a smile. "I think Hulda heard that something besides sex was the motive, but she couldn't come up with the right word."

"Sheila copied something or stole the rights to something?" I asked.

"Maybe she misrepresented her ownership," Howard replied.

I thought about my trips through the 4-H quilt displays and the comments I'd heard day-after-day about the judging, the biases that should, or should not, have come into play when comparing the crafts. Sheila's quilt had won third place, and to my eye was far superior to the quality of any quilt that fell lower in the judge's rankings. Third place was hardly taking the grand prize, or even second place.

"Sheila had a quilt that took third place at the fair," I said.

"So what?" Scooter asked. "That 4-H stuff is just for the kids. I don't even know why they let adults compete."

I looked to Howard for a comment. After a few moments of thought he asked, "How would you plagiarize a quilt? Did she steal a pattern from someone?"

"It was a bassoon design with notes coming out of the bell," I replied. "There wasn't anything else like it."

"Ahem," I heard and turned to see who was behind me. Nancy, the director, was giving me a menacing look.

"Just taking a break," I replied, getting up from the table and drinking down the last of my coffee.

"Sheila O'Keefe has been trying to reach you," Nancy said as we walked out of the dining room. "When the receptionist kept getting your voicemail, she asked me to track you down and pass on the message. She handed me a Post-it note with Sheila's name and cell phone number. " Without breaking stride, Nancy added, "I don't suppose Sheila has a business-related issue."

"She's in the City Band and I'm sure it's something related to tomorrow's concert. By the way, there has been a lot of buzz about me filling in as the director and it's getting Whistling Pines a lot of good press." I hoped that would resonate well with the director, who liked Whistling Pines to get free advertising.

Chapter 24

I tried Sheila's cell phone number and it rolled over to voicemail where I left a message saying I was returning her call.

As soon as I hung up the phone rang again. The caller ID said Howard Chapman was calling and it took me two rings to realize that Jenny's father was on the line. I'd never spoken to him other than at the restaurant.

"Mr. Chapman, how are you?"

"First of all, please call me Howard. Second, you should come over for supper tonight." Howard reacted to my speechlessness as reluctance and added, "Barbara is making a Yankee pot roast and it's the best meal she makes, other than her Thanksgiving turkey dinner."

"Pot roast is one of my favorites and I haven't had it since I was a kid. I'd love to have dinner with you."

"We eat early, so why don't you come over at five and we'll have a drink while Barbara finishes off the side dishes."

"Can I bring a bottle of wine?" I asked.

"You don't need to bring anything but your appetite," Howard replied.

As soon as Howard hung up, I called Anderson's flower shop and ordered an arrangement of whatever looked best and could be ready for pick up before my trip to the Chapman home.

The rest of the afternoon flew by in a blur without a return call from Sheila. I expected Jenny to stop by and explain the sudden dinner offer, but she never appeared.

Jenny had a cubicle in the corner of the relatively large health center where she and five other nurses and aides managed the medical needs of the residents. That ranged from maintaining medical files on the most independent residents to administering drugs for those incapable of managing their own scheduled medications.

Jenny was studying a file when I cleared my throat. She put her finger on the page to keep her place, then turned.

"Hi," she said. "What's up?"

"I'm going home to put on a clean shirt, then I'll see you for supper."

"I don't think supper will work tonight. Jeremy has a math test tomorrow and we need to do a lot of review."

"Your father called a little while ago and invited me over for Yankee pot roast."

Jenny stared at me for a few seconds, awaiting some sign that I wasn't serious.

"He said to be at the house at five because you eat early," I added.

"Amazing," Jenny said. "I was going to stay late because the gerontologist was here today and I have a pile charts to update with his notes. Dad picks tonight to invite you over for dinner. I guess no one thought to ask me if it was okay to invite my boyfriend over."

"I'm sorry," I said. "I could've run down right after he called to give you a 'heads up' but I thought you were probably in on the planning."

Jenny slammed the chart, a three-ring red binder, closed and slipped it into a pigeonhole over her desk. "I suppose I should run home so I can change into something that's not splattered with blood, sputum, and heaven knows what other bodily fluids." She took a key ring from her pocket and locked her desk and the gray steel case above her desk where narcotics were stored.

"Look, if this is a problem I can call and trump up an excuse," I said, backpedaling as Jenny stepped out of her cubicle.

"It's not your problem, Peter. Come on over. Maybe you can even help Jeremy. Long division was never my strong suit."

Chapter 25

I arrived at the Chapman doorstep with a mountain of anxiety. I was reaching for the doorbell when the door swung open and Barbara appeared. She looked at the flowers and I pushed them toward her.

"Thanks for the dinner invitation," I said, presenting the flowers to her.

"Oh dear," she said accepting the flowers and tilting her head to examine the bouquet. "This is so large it won't work as a centerpiece. It would interfere with conversation. I'll have to put them on the sideboard." She started to turn and then looked over her shoulder to say, "Thank you. They're very pretty." As an afterthought she added, "Howard is in the dining room."

Overhead I heard galloping and within seconds Jeremy was hurtling down the stairs. He raced past me and looked around the floor. "Where's your guitar?" he asked.

"I didn't bring it in."

"Go get it. I want you to show Grandpa that riff you played for me. The one you said The Doors did for 'Light My Fire.'" When I hesitated he said, "Never mind, I'll get it for you," and he flew out the door toward my car.

"In here!" Howard called from a room down the hallway.

I slipped off my shoes and was in the dining room when Jeremy slammed the front door and came racing in behind me as I was shaking hands with Jenny's father. The dining room was big enough for a comfortable dinner with a dozen people. The furniture was dark oak that stood on the same plush white carpeting as in the hallway. The room smelled of furniture polish and trails from recent vacuuming tracked the carpet, making me feel even more sure that having me over for dinner had caused Barbara a great deal of trouble.

Howard handed me a low-ball glass with two ice cubes and dark liquid. "A little bird told me that you enjoy Jack Daniels so I picked up a bottle this afternoon." There was a small fold-out bar against one wall and Howard picked up a martini glass with clear liquid and an olive from the marble bar top. "Cheers!" he said, lifting his glass to mine.

I took a sip of the unusually smooth whiskey. I looked at the bottle and saw it wasn't the typical Jack Daniels I bought but was an 18-year-old Special Reserve, the kind that was kept in a locked case in the liquor store. The cost was way over my budget and the fine aged liquor was better quality than my palate could appreciate, although I was touched by the gesture.

Jeremy had put my guitar case on the floor in a corner of the room and he was quickly releasing the latches. He gently took the guitar out of the case and held it like it was something magical. He carefully crossed the room with it and held it out to me, explaining to Jenny's father, "It's a Martin acoustic six-string, the same kind that professional musicians use when they make their un-plugged albums."

"I don't know that your grandpa wants a music session right now, Jeremy," I said, gently taking the guitar from him and holding it by the neck.

"We have a little time before supper's ready," Howard said, taking my glass. "Go ahead and play something."

I sat in a high-backed chair and tuned for a few seconds and then asked, "What would you like to hear? If I've heard it, I can usually play it."

"Yeah, Grandpa, Peter said that he sat around nights in Iraq just playing whatever the Marines wanted to hear. He can play anything."

"Can you play something from the '60s?" Howard asked.

I played the guitar riff from "American Woman," by the Guess Who and then slid into "Classical Gas," an instrumental piece written and recorded by Mason Williams. When I ended, Howard's mouth was agape. "Wow," he said.

I looked up. Jenny was standing at the dining room door. She'd changed into white shorts and a pink T-shirt. I could tell she was pleased that I'd impressed her father. "Play 'Autumn Leaves'" she said.

I'd played a few bars when Barbara rushed into the room with tears in her eyes, stopping at the door and looking like she'd seen a ghost. I stopped and we all stared at her for a second. She motioned for me to keep playing, then slid under Howard's arm as I restarted. I'd never seen her face express any emotion, yet she was sobbing into a tissue by the time I finished the second verse. Unsure what I'd caused, I got up, set the guitar in the case and was shocked when I turned around and she hugged me, staining my shirt with tears.

Without releasing the hug she said, "My brother was killed in Viet Nam. The night before he left he sat on the porch and played that song to his girlfriend while I hid in the living room and listened." Barbara stepped back and held me by my shoulders. "Mom caught me sitting there and made me go to bed. He was on the van to Minneapolis before I got up the next morning. I never got to say goodbye to him. My last memory is him strumming his guitar and singing that song to Mary."

A buzzer sounded in the kitchen and Barbara quickly left. Howard joined her to cut the roast while Jeremy and I helped Jenny fill water glasses from a crystal decanter.

While Jeremy was on the opposite side of the table I whispered, "That was really odd. Did you know that would happen when you asked me to play that song?"

"Mom told me the story about hearing her brother singing to his girlfriend and she'd mentioned 'Autumn Leaves.' I knew it might be special for her, but I didn't expect the waterworks."

I remembered sitting in the barracks with a dozen Marines singing along to songs they requested. I played the guitar and told some jokes to help everyone "decompress" from the daily grind of driving around, making contact with the locals while constantly worrying about being blown to pieces by an IED under the next pile of rocks along the road. All of us were on edge all the time and playing video games or guitar were about the only breaks from the harsh reality of life in the blowing sand.

"Hello! Earth calling Peter," Jenny said, bringing me back to the dining room. "Supper will be on the table shortly."

"Sorry," I said. Jenny handed me two crystal red wine glasses and I set them on the table.

Howard delivered the pot roast on a huge platter surrounded by potatoes, carrots, and pearl onions. Barbara, who had removed all of her tear-stained makeup, came in with a gravy boat. I took the gravy boat from her and set it on the table. She was standing uncomfortably close to me when I straightened up. Barbara put her hand on my bicep, pulled me close and kissed my cheek, whispering, "Thank you," in my ear.

I said, "It was my pleasure," realizing it was the first time I'd ever seen her without makeup and I could see how much Jenny resembled her.

Jenny poured red wine into glasses for the adults while Jeremy dove into the pot roast platter, spearing the largest piece along with several browned potatoes. As we ate, Barbara showed a soft, funny side I'd never seen before. She seemed like a different person and laughed out loud when Jeremy tried to tell a knock-knock joke and botched the punch line. I wondered if she'd been nipping the cooking sherry.

"Your mother is very colorful," Barbara said, politely understating her true feelings about Mother. "Will we see her at the band concert tomorrow night?"

"I haven't told her about it." I managed to filter my first thought; I was glad she wasn't coming. I didn't need the drama when I was already stressed to the limit.

"I could give her a call," Barbara offered.

"That would be nice," I replied, trying to sound upbeat while my stomach churned. "But my mother's life is usually full and she doesn't respond well to disruptions to her routine."

"I doubt that she'd miss another performance of her son as the band director. I'll give her a call in the morning," Barbara said.

Jenny studied my face for a reaction, but I managed to suppress the grimace I was feeling. "I won't have much time to socialize," I countered.

"That's okay," Howard said. "We'll bring an extra chair and we'll keep her entertained until the concert is over."

"Thanks," was all I could say.

We made small talk by talking about my arrival in Two Harbors, Jenny's growing up in Two Harbors, and Jeremy's struggles with math homework. Howard loved his job and made enough money that Barbara was able to be a stay-at-home mom and grandmother who took pride in keeping the house spotless, the gardens weed free, and the lawn manicured. Every aspect of their lives was orderly and neat. It was the exact opposite of life growing up with my mother, which was controlled chaos with a house in disarray, a garden overgrown with weeds, and a lawn that was patchy and always in need of mowing. I looked at Jenny and wondered if people from such different worlds could ever be happy together.

The doorbell rang as we were clearing the table and Jeremy ran to answer it while the rest of us carried dishes to the kitchen, contrary to the insistence of Barbara who wanted them left so she could deal with them after "the company" was gone. I was walking back to the dining room when Jeremy came nearly running down the hallway with a brown-haired girl in tow.

"Peter, Abby Finch is here to see you," he declared, pulling her forward and almost pushing her into my arms. "She wants to talk to you about the piccolo part of the concert."

Poor Abby, with her plain, acne-covered face turning bright red, swatted at Jeremy's hand when he tried to push her toward me. "Um, Mister Rogers, um, I was, um, wondering if you, um, could help me, um, with the piccolo part, um, of the march." She hesitated for a second and then added softly, "but if you're busy, I'll just go home and practice some more."

I waved her into the dining room and asked her to take the piccolo out of the case. While she did that, I took out my guitar. "Run through a scale for me," I said, and then I followed her notes with the guitar. She was a little sharp, so we talked through a tiny twist to get on pitch, and then did the scale again.

"Now, I'll play a few bars leading up to the piccolo solo, and then you play the solo while I play the tuba part on guitar in the background," I said. I was suddenly aware that the household had gathered at the dining room door. I played a few bars, but Abby was a half beat late starting her solo. I let her play through it and I stopped playing after she ended her trill.

"That was pretty good," I said. "You need to catch the downbeat to start the solo and then hold the trill at the end for a full four beats." She nodded and turned to leave.

"Wait, we're going to do it again," I said. I played the same opening bars and this time she was right on the beat and she held the trill. "Perfect!" I said. Jenny clapped and suddenly there was a round of applause and Abby blushed.

"Are you all set now?" I asked.

Abby shook her head. "I don't want to play it alone. I won't do a solo. If no one plays with me, I'm not coming to the concert."

I could see the determination, or maybe stage fright, in her eyes. She said, "Mrs. Karvonen told me she gave you a piccolo a couple days ago, but everyone in the school band says you can't learn to play a piccolo in a few days. They keep telling me that this is my big chance to shine, but I don't want to be embarrassed in front of the whole town. I told Mr. Johnson, the tuba player, to make sure you had the music." Although she said it softly, her determination showed through her nervousness.

"Can I borrow your piccolo?" I asked.

She readily handed it to me and I drew a deep breath before playing the whole piccolo part of "Stars and Stripes Forever." Abby and Jenny's whole family were silent when I finished. I handed the piccolo back to Abby and asked, "Did I do okay?"

She broke into a shy smile and took her piccolo back. "You're pretty good. I bet you've been playing piccolo longer than four days."

"Lots longer," I lied. "Are we ready for a piccolo duet tomorrow night?"

I got a silent nod and she re-cased the piccolo before she let Jeremy take her back to the front door.

Howard came over and clapped me on the back. "I would never have dreamt that someone could play 'Stars and Stripes Forever' on a guitar."

"Any song is just a string of notes and if you can play the notes, you can play the song." I played the opening bars of the "Tennessee Waltz" and let that morph into "The Piano Man." Howard and Barbara were rapt. Jenny stood back and smiled while I impressed her parents.

"You could be professional," Barbara said.

"I am professional," I replied. "Whistling Pines pays me to put on programs and part of that job is playing guitar or piano."

"But," Barbara started. I cut her off.

"There are a few musicians who make good money, but most of them work at it part time and have some other job, like waiting tables or tending bar to pay the rent," I explained. "I get to make a living and play some music too. It's about perfect."

Jenny slid between her parents and gave me a hug. It was a flagrant public display of affection for her subdued family, but both Howard and Barbara smiled. Barbara had let her guard down in front of me. That was proven when I packed up my guitar and went to the front door. After I tied my shoes, Barbara did what I once regarded as "the unthinkable." She gave me another quick hug. Not close. Not for more than one second. But our relationship was obviously forever changed.

Jenny walked with me to the car and pulled me close after I'd put the guitar in the back seat. "I think you got a new fan tonight," she said before giving me a lingering kiss.

"Your mom let her guard down."

"I don't think there are five people outside the immediate family who've ever seen my mother without her makeup. You are in the honored minority." She hesitated and then added, "or else you're part of the family."

There was an unspoken question with the comment and the whole evening had me a little mentally off-balance. I was shaken by Barbara's sudden transformation, and Howard had made it clear through his warmth and actions that he was ready to accept me. Jeremy was, well, himself, a typical harebrained kid who seemed to respect and appreciate me. I was about to suggest that we go shopping for a diamond ring once the concert was behind me when the mood was broken.

"Mom!" Jeremy yelled from the front door, "I'm stuck on problem four. Just kiss him and come help me."

Jenny knew something had changed, too. She stepped on her tiptoes and gave me a warm, slow kiss. It wasn't our usual peck and good-bye, nor was it a high-school French kiss with probing tongues that weren't quite sure where to go. It was more of a I-love-you-dearly-and-we-really-don't-need-to-indulge-in-childish-gyrations-anymore kiss.

She squeezed my hand and put her head against my shoulder. "I want to have a baby with you someday." Then she pushed away and I saw a twinkle in her eye that made me wonder if she'd said it just because she knew that comment alone would keep me from sleeping.

Chapter 26

Thursday

I was still full of pot roast when I awoke, so I went through my morning shave and shower routine and jumped into the car without making coffee or eating breakfast. Wendy was already working on a crossword puzzle when I got to the dining room. Barbie was carefully pulling petunias out of a linen bag and arranging them in vases on the tables. I wondered if they were from her own garden.

Angie Lafond came crashing through the kitchen door looking for someone. Her eyes locked on me and she stalked over. "Someone has to deal with Miriam," she demanded.

I was torn between asking why she was telling me about it, or saying something flippant, when I sensed her seriousness. "What's the problem?" I asked.

"She keeps having these hot flashes and she stops whatever she's doing and runs into the freezer."

"How is that a big problem?"

Angie let out a sigh. "Don't you understand? The kitchen is like a machine with all the parts working together.

If you have a part that keeps running into the freezer to cool off, the other parts get out of sync."

"But you're the head cook," I protested. "Why don't you talk to her?"

"Because I have to keep working with her, and she likes you better." Angie quickly disappeared into the kitchen. Now I really needed coffee.

"Peter," Wendy yelled from the far side of the dining room. "I need a three-letter word for a Turkish hat."

"F-E-Z" I replied.

Miriam flew out of the kitchen like a rocket. "Angie said you wanted to talk to me about some problem." There was fire in her eyes and I set my cup down and hung my head.

I steered her toward the door leading to the lawn. Wendy and Barbie were both trying to look suspiciously disinterested. As we passed through the door I could see the pink rising on Miriam's neck. She suddenly shed her apron and opened the top buttons of her white blouse. She started flapping the apron like a fan.

"Hot flash?" I asked.

"They're driving me nuts! I get hot and sweat, then I get chilled. The only thing that helps is running into the walk-in freezer until they pass."

"Actually, that's what Angie wanted me to talk to you about. You're disrupting the flow."

"Disrupting the flow! She doesn't want me stripping off clothes or sweating all over the food, so I don't have any option except sticking my head in the freezer." Miriam paced as she ranted.

"Tell me about Sheila O'Keefe," I suggested, changing the topic.

"What's to tell? She's an oversexed exhibitionist who has a reputation that would embarrass a two-bit whore."

"Is her reputation real?"

"What's real in this small town is whatever people think is real," Miriam replied.

"Miriam, you're the one person I can trust to give me an honest answer that's not slanted by opinion. What do you really know about Sheila?"

Miriam became pensive and stared at me as if she was deciding how much she could trust me. "This is a true tidbit, and I'll share it with you only because I know you'll never repeat it." She waited until I'd nodded assent. "Sheila has two sides: She has all the flashy outfits, the toned and tanned body, and flirts with the men in town. The other side of Sheila is very quiet and secretive. She lives in a big old house on the east end of Duluth with a high fence and a gated driveway."

"Other than the price of a house like that, I guess it doesn't surprise me too much," I said.

"Sheila lives with a girlfriend."

"I suppose that makes some sense, just from a safety standpoint," I replied.

Miriam gave me the "slow child" look. "Her girlfriend is her life partner. The heterosexual stuff with the guys is just bluster."

I was skeptical. "How would you know that?"

"Craig and I took a trip to Branson, Missouri, a couple years ago. We stayed in an EconoLodge and every morning I'd see this nice, pretty girl coming out of the room next to ours and we'd chat while we walked down to the continental breakfast buffet. She'd pick up a couple rolls and coffee and take them back to her room. The walls were a little thin and every night we'd hear her howling like a beagle while she was in the throes of ecstasy. One evening we came back from a show at the Andy Williams Theater and there was the pretty little thing walking arm and arm down the motel hallway with Sheila.

"Sheila wasn't sure who we were at first, but at some point over the next couple days her friend told her that we were from Minnesota and she must've connected us to Two Harbors. The next time I saw Sheila, she steered me into a ladies room and begged me not to 'out' her."

"And you haven't?"

"I haven't, and neither will you. I have a few skeletons in my closet, so I understand and respect her wishes. The only reason I'm telling you is because this whole stupid thing about her getting poisoned is getting way out of hand. There are some suspicious wives, and some lecherous men who have ideas, but Sheila hasn't been bedding or stealing any husbands. She flirts and flatters, but she doesn't go beyond. You can bank on that."

With this sudden new perspective on Sheila, I went back to my office with a whole new range of motives, from scorned girlfriends to someone who got "outed" because of her association with Sheila. The poisoning fit better with a female attacker, and this news about Sheila's sexual orientation suddenly seemed quite pertinent.

As soon as I sat down Wendy blew into my office. "I've been thinking about plagiarism," she said as she edged me out of the desk chair. She sat down, entered my not-so-secret password and then pulled up "thesaurus.com." and entered the word "plagiarize." A page popped up with the proper pronunciation, saying it is a verb, and the definition: To forge. Following that were a list of synonyms. I stood behind her looking over her shoulder, reading the list. "Fake, forge, copy, mimeograph, mirror, reflect, Xerox, steal, use, and usurp" were listed with dozens of others.

"Hulda had the word wrong, but did she have the meaning right?" I asked. "Sometimes she gets a homophone that sounds right but means something totally different, like when she said philatelist but meant philanderer."

Wendy's fingers hovered over the keyboard before pulling up Google and searching for homophones of plagiarize. "There's nothing here except some short phrases that end with eyes: Lying eyes, Evil eyes. Oh wait, here's Simonize. Do you think Sheila Simonized someone?"

"I doubt it, but I don't even know what Simonize means."

Again her fingers flew over the keys. "Simonize – To polish a car or to apply wax to a car. Do you think she polished someone?" Wendy gave me a suggestive leer. "Maybe she just polished one part of someone, or someone's husband. Maybe she botched someone's wax job."

"Am I interrupting something?" The question came from a third voice.

I spun around and found Nancy standing at my door. "No, we're just trying to figure out what Hulda Packer meant when she said someone had plagiarized something."

"Why don't you ask her when you drive the van to Betty's Pies? She's sitting in the front row of the van waiting for a driver."

I looked at my watch and realized I was five minutes late for the Thursday afternoon field trip to the pie shop. It was a popular event and we always had a van filled with people looking forward to the outing. I sprinted for the front lobby, leaving Wendy to explain why she was sitting at my computer reading the thesaurus webpage. I was sure Wendy would come up with a plausible explanation that would implicate me and exonerate her.

The trip to Betty's Pies was pure chaos and I never got a chance to talk with Hulda about Sheila's plagiarizing. Betty's was very busy and we had to split the group among several tables spread throughout the restaurant. I was forced to walk back and forth, assisting with menu choices, finding lost reading glasses, searching for a lost wallet, and helping an octogenarian to the bathroom.

By the time we got back to Whistling Pines and unloaded, it was time for me to drive home, change into my white and black outfit, then rush to the bandshell. I closed the door to my office as the sweet smell of Honey Cavendish tobacco wafted around me.

"I'm really in a hurry, Len," I said without the need to look.

"I heard Tinker Oldham was moved out of the ICU today, so I stopped in to see if he remembered anything about the afternoon he was bumped," Len said, fiddling with his unlit pipe. "A funny thing happened while I was there. A teenaged kid showed up with a bouquet of flowers he'd picked from his mother's garden. He stammered through an explanation of shooting the rubber-band at the bull without looking up and handed Tinker an apology note. His father was standing behind him and nudged him. The kid was sweating bullets and staring at his shoes, but he told Tinker that when his 4-H calf sold he'd pay for the hospital costs Medicare didn't cover."

"Interesting story," I said, checking my watch to make sure I still had plenty of time to make it home and change.

"I talked with the father who told me about some young guy with a crew cut who figured out what had happened and confronted his son. I got the feeling the kid's sudden remorse had something to do with you."

I couldn't help but smile.

"Are you going to tell the sheriff you solved the bull kicking crime?" Len asked.

"I don't see any point," I said, checking my watch again. "It seems like justice has been served."

"If the sheriff ever finds out you solved the case and his department didn't get credit for solving the crime, he'll be pissed."

"Are you going to tell him?" I asked.

Len fiddled with his pipe, then put the stem in his mouth. "It's not my place to say anything to him, and I doubt the kid will either."

"Then the case is closed."

Len was smiling and shaking his head as I rushed for the parking lot.

Chapter 27

I found a parking spot on the block behind the bandshell and said hello to the musicians who were filtering across the park. The doors leading to the storage room beneath the stage floor were open. I walked down the narrow steps to the basement storage area and headed toward the cacophony of voices and the clatter of instrument cases and folding chairs. I was unsurprised to find Brian Johnson regaling the group of middle-aged musicians with tuba jokes. He delivered his punch line and rushed over to shake my hand.

"Doc, glad you made it a little early. There are some things you need to deal with."

"I'd prefer Peter to being called Doc."

"Whatever you prefer, but word has been circulating that your nickname is Doc, Doc," Brian said as he led me back up the stairs and onto the stage. "We have a shortage of chairs."

I looked at the stage and the three rows of chairs. "I don't understand."

"We put out all the chairs and there aren't enough for all the musicians," Brian explained. "We're short three chairs."

"Are you missing some?"

"Not really. It's just that a few of them are old and a little shaky, and we're getting an unprecedented number of alumni members for the year-end concert."

"What are alumni members?"

"Your name is entered in a log book before your first practice with the band. That makes you an official band member until your obituary appears in the *Lake County News-Chronicle*. When you move away or stop playing, you become an inactive alumnus, but we welcome back anyone who has an instrument and wants to play."

Not having time to process the information I pointed at the Lutheran church across the street. "Find a couple of the younger members and borrow chairs from the church."

Brian led me back down the stairs and introduced me to Pastor Ralph Kitteson. "Pastor, we'd like to borrow chairs to seat the extra alumni who showed up for tonight's concert."

The pastor tapped a couple of the teen band members "The back door isn't locked. We need three chairs." He turned back and asked, "Is there anything else I can do?"

I smiled. "What instrument do you play, Pastor?"

"I play this battered old clarinet," he said, holding up his instrument for my inspection.

I took it gently and turned it from end to end noting a few dings. "I've never seen this construction before, but based on my education, I'd guess this is BTR."

The pastor was smiling as I passed the clarinet back to him. He said, "You're probably the only other person in Two Harbors who can recognize Bithermal Reinforced Grendilla. I suppose you also recognize the Kanstul tuba that Brian Johnson plays."

I watched as Brian gently lifted his tuba from its case. Unlike most of the other brass instruments that had a slight patina from age, the tuba reflected like a mirror with a slight reddish hue. Brian handed it to me.

"Kanstul is a relatively new company in Anaheim, California, that has rediscovered the value of adding a little more copper to their brass, which gives the instrument a little mellower sound." I was impressed, knowing that the modern mass-produced instruments played notes, but the older instruments, or those made from old technology, added a special resonance to their music.

"Play your heart out, Brian," I said, then headed for the stairs.

Outside I found John Carr leaning against a tree behind the bandshell. "John, I'd like to take you into my confidence."

"Don't sweat it, Peter," he said. "You'll do fine tonight. The band is well rehearsed and you'll be proud of us."

I smiled. "Thank you, but I have another issue."

I looked around and saw dozens of people carrying folding lawn chairs and blankets. Miriam and her husband were setting up lawn chairs near an old cannon in the middle of the park, and Tucker, the homely dog she'd adopted after his Whistling Pines owner died, was sniffing the wheels of the cannon before lifting his leg on it. That done, he found a black lab puppy a few feet away and the two of them started tumbling in the grass, nipping at each other's ears. Everywhere there were old neighbors reconnecting and children playing: I had an overwhelming feeling I'd become part of the community.

Near the east end of the bandshell a string of older women were dragging old wooden lawn chairs across the grass. As they set them up I saw Dolores, who gave me a discreet nod. They sat and although the evening was still warm they spread blankets and crocheted afghans across their laps. A few musicians were by the bandshell door smoking their last cigarettes before the concert.

"John, I'm worried about Sheila O'Keefe. I'm afraid someone might try to hurt her again tonight."

"Oh my," he replied. "Have there been threats?"

"I'm not aware of any specific threats, but whoever arranged the first attack is still out there. You sit next to her. Please keep an eye on her."

"I'm uniquely prepared for that responsibility," he said, sliding back the tail of his jacket. Hanging on his belt was a pistol in a holster. "I have a concealed carry permit for my gun."

"I don't think you'll have to shoot anyone or throw your body in front of her. Just make sure someone doesn't slip another peanut into her reed case."

"You don't think that wasn't just a terrible practical joke?" he asked, letting the jacket slide over the holster, disguising it well.

"There are a few theories and most make me believe the attack was more than that. Sheila has more detractors than supporters and I think someone took their dislike for her a little too far."

"She's a bit of an enigma," John replied. "As the director, I am like a counselor for some of the musicians. Sheila and I have had a few discussions. Two Harbors isn't a friendly place for her. I think she may have moved to Duluth after one of our heart-to-heart discussions. It's hard to live an alternative lifestyle in a small town."

John gave me a knowing look and I admitted, "Yes, I know she's a lesbian. On the other hand, I think that secret is well guarded and probably not what's behind this."

The clatter of footsteps on the stairs, chairs scraping, and the sounds of instrument tuning started behind us. John glanced at his watch, "Show time," he said, limping up the steps with one hand on my shoulder and the other on his alto saxophone. At the top of the stairs he paused and straightened up. "You worry about the band. Sheila is in my safe hands for tonight."

We walked to the bandshell and I made a quick search of the stage and wings, looking for Sheila. Abby, my fellow piccoloist, seated between the two flutists, gave me a nervous wave. I patted my pocket, to show her that I had the piccolo and realized I'd left it at home.

Jenny's family was seated near the street in a row of captain's chairs and I tried to get her attention by waving discreetly. When that failed, I flailed my arms, and quickly realized that the conversation they were having with the family sitting next to them was more absorbing, so I leaped down from the stage and ran across the park, dodging chairs, children, and a daschund who wanted to playfully grab my pants cuff.

"Jenny," I said breathlessly, "I need you to drive back to my house and get the piccolo from the kitchen table."

"But the concert starts in like three minutes."

I pointed my thumb over my shoulder. "I know, but Abby Finch expects me to play a piccolo duet with her in the last song." I turned and watched Abby talking excitedly with the flutists on the stage.

"Aw, crap," Jenny said, gathering her linen bag. "Jeremy, stay with Grandpa and Grandma."

Sheila was climbing the stairs to the stage, her bassoon hanging from a strap around her neck. She was dressed in black slacks and a white blouse that was less revealing than her outfit from the county fair, but still left a lot of cleavage showing. She looked older and I realized she wasn't wearing any makeup except for some subdued lipstick.

"I'm so glad you're here," I said, giving her a hug that was returned without enthusiasm.

"I'm not sure this is a good idea," she said, giving me a sad look, "but I have a new EpiPen in my pocket and I thought I'd give it a try." She joined the band and selected a reed before tuning with the band. I noticed she kept careful control of her reed cases. John Carr leaned over and patted her on the arm. In return he got a half-hearted smile.

Abby Finch was giving me nervous glances after watching my sprint into the crowd. I gave her a reassuring smile and a thumbs-up. She blushed and quickly looked away.

I stepped to the podium and rapped my director's baton on the edge, bringing the band to silence. I nodded to each of the band sections and got a nod in return indicating everyone's readiness. I took the microphone and faced the crowd.

"Good evening, ladies and gentlemen, and welcome to the Two Harbors City Band year-end concert. I'm Peter Rogers, and although I'm a relative newcomer to town, I've been offered the honor of filling in as the guest director. As most of you know, our final concert is always an all-march evening. Judging by the size of the crowd and the number of alumni members who've joined us, I'd say it's very popular.

"Without further delay, I'd like to introduce the 'Washington Post March,' by John Phillip Sousa." I raised the baton and the band members brought up their instruments." With the first down stroke the band hit the opening note. I was immediately energized. We moved on to the "Colonel Bogey March" by Kenneth Alford; the traditional marching song "The British Grenadiers;" and then back to Sousa with "Semper Fidelis." The band played with flawless precision and I was carried to a euphoric world of harmony.

A fast forty-five minutes later we took a ten-minute intermission. I looked frantically for Jenny, but her chair was still empty. While scanning the crowd, I found a group of gray-headed attendees sitting near the corner of the park. I recognized many of the Whistling Pines residents chatting among themselves, along with a few other senior citizens. Wendy moved among them like a mother hen. I saw Jenny's mother, Barbara, who gave me a regal nod when our eyes met, which gave me a rush when I again realized that Jenny was still nowhere in sight with the piccolo.

I checked with Sheila, who was sitting stonily in her chair next to John Carr, carefully holding her reed cases. "Are you doing okay?" I asked.

John Carr leaned close and held Sheila's elbow. "We're fine," he replied, staying true to his promise to keep an eye on her. As he leaned, his coat slid aside and I saw his holster, which gave me a feeling of confidence that he did have control of whatever situation might arise.

We opened the second set with a song called "The Viva Mexico March" and cruised through three more numbers before I had another chance to look for Jenny. She wasn't in her chair and my heart fell.

We were down to the last three songs when I announced "The Triumphal March" by Verdi. I flipped open the music and saw the bassoon solo and nodded to Sheila. She looked confident and took a deep breath. The song opened with the trumpet fanfare and the rest of the band followed. I was again floating with the music and saw the bassoon solo approaching. Sheila stood and started her solo when a rim shot rang out. None were in the music. I glanced at the drummer who was also looking around. I kept directing, but glanced at the audience over my shoulder just as I heard a scream and saw a woman running toward the stage with a pistol. I realized the rim shot I'd heard was actually a gunshot.

I looked quickly at Sheila, who looked shocked, but was behind John Carr. His Glock pistol was out of its holster and his body was between Sheila and the shooter. He edged her toward the stairs with the gun at his side.

I looked around and the world seemed to be in slow motion. The crowd was in chaos with screams, crying, and yelling as people scrambled from their chairs. To my great relief, I saw Jenny's family, still in the back of the crowd, safely behind the shooter and slowly moving behind the row of cars parked along the street. Through the cacophony I heard Miriam yelling, "NO, Tucker! No!" I saw Tucker running as fast as a half basset/half St. Bernard can run toward the shooter, baying a sorrowful moan and looking like Dumbo about to take wing on the strength of his flapping ears.

Motion at the corner below the bandstand caught my eye and I saw Dolores struggling to get free of the afghan covering her lap. My instincts were torn between trying to stop the advancing woman with the gun, or jumping down to protect Dolores. Before I had to make the decision, a gun barrel appeared from under the afghan, but the breach was tangled in the loose weave. "Uh oh," was all I could say.

While still tangled in the afghan, Dolores' gun belched white smoke. The concussion echoed in the bandshell. I heard lead pellets from the errant shot buzz past my ear like a swarm of bees. Above me a piece of the bandshell exploded as Dolores' shot blew splinters into the air, some of them raining down on the band. Until that point, remnants of the music had continued, but as the splinters rained down, the music died and the musicians scrambled for the exits as the sulfurous white smoke drifted across the stage. In the background I heard Miriam calling Tucker.

The woman racing through the crowd with the gun became disoriented by the noise and smoke generated from the blunderbuss' black powder. She stopped at the edge of the bandshell and Tucker bit the cuff of her jeans. The chaos, the white smoke, the band members scrambling from their chairs, and John Carr's human shield, made it impossible for her to identify Sheila from all the other white and black clad musicians. I jumped from the stage and tackled the woman as screams continued to emanate from the fleeing crowd.

Fearing the discharge of another load of buckshot, I looked to the edge of the stage. Dolores freed the old, short-barreled blunderbuss, once called a lap gun because they'd been carried for protection on the laps of people traveling in horse-drawn coaches. It had only one barrel and needed to be reloaded after reach shot, so no one else was in peril from Dolores.

The shooter was a hefty woman dressed in denim jeans and a t-shirt. Even with my running tackle she hadn't gone down easily. Once she was on the ground several spectators wrestled her gun away and I held her until Len Rentz took over. On the ground, and without her gun, the wind was out of her sails and she sat on the ground sobbing.

"That bitch stole my pink ribbon," she blubbered. "She didn't sew that quilt; she bought it in Branson! She has no right! My quilt should be going to the State Fair."

With Len in control, I rushed for the stage to check on Sheila and anyone else who might've been hit by the gunshots or flying debris. I found a number of band members still on the stage amazingly calm, mostly just taking in the crazy scene in the crowd, while others had sought shelter in the bandshell basement. I pulled myself onto the stage and found Sheila sitting in the back corner of the bandshell, sobbing into John Carr's shoulder.

I threaded my way through the band members and knelt beside her. "Are you okay?"

"I'm fine," she said with resignation. "The bullet missed me."

I looked around and no one seemed to be bleeding or injured. "Is everyone OK?" I shouted. When no one responded, I asked, "Does anyone know where the bullet went?"

"Dang it!" I heard from the back of the bandshell. Pushing my way back through the toppled chairs I found Brian Johnson poking his little finger through the bell of his tuba. "I just bought this! It's my E-flat, 4-valve Kanstul! Why didn't I bring my Martin Renowned Monster? I wouldn't care if there was a bullet hole in my Martin."

I let out a sigh of relief, seeing the bullet lodged high in the back wall of the bandshell. "I'm sure it can be repaired," I said. "I'm just glad no one was hurt."

"Repair it?" Brian asked, regaining his composure. "Are you kidding? Can you imagine the stories I can tell every time I pull this out of the case? There's got to be a new tuba joke here somewhere."

"But you can't play it like that."

"You don't know tubas," Brian replied. "Like I told you before, a pinhole will make a trumpet useless, but a bullet hole won't affect a tuba." To demonstrate, he played a few bars of the "The Beer Barrel Polka."

Jenny pushed her way through the musicians and pulled me close. After the hug she pushed me back and said, "You're a mess!" I looked down and saw that my shirt was grass-stained and my bloody knee was poking through a hole in my pant leg.

"Hey, Doc," Brian said, "it looks like you deserve another purple heart."

I ignored him and went back to check on the rest of the band with Jenny in tow. We determined that no one was suffering from angina or any other ailments more severe than bruises from flying chairs and music stands. A few people had splinters in their hair from the ceiling. I felt a tug at my elbow and found myself facing Abby Finch's pimpled face.

"Mister Rogers, are we going to play the last song?" she asked with the piccolo in her hand.

I looked at the carnage on the stage, the mixture of overturned chairs, wood splinters, scattered sheet music, an abandoned trombone with a bent slide, and a couple broken folding chairs. "I think everyone is too upset," I said.

That comment was followed by grumbling from the band members who were now picking up the carnage. "The show must go on!" someone shouted from the back row. I felt something hard in my hand and saw the piccolo case Jenny pressed into my palm. She leaned close and whispered, "They're right. The show must go on. Don't disappoint Abby or your audience." Her tone of voice made it clear this was non-negotiable.

I walked to the center of the carnage and to the band members I said, "Let's wrap up the set."

Brian Johnson helped the band reassemble the jumbled chairs and music stands while I rounded up the rest of the band members.

The band took their seats, other than Sheila who left the stage under John Carr's care. It took a few minutes to sort the music, but we got it all together. By the time everyone was settled the shadows were getting long.

I found the microphone and walked to the middle of the stage. "I've never heard of a gunshot in a concert except for cannons in the '1812 Overture'," I said, garnering a few laughs from the crowd, who had mostly found their way back to the park. "I understand the band has played "Stars and Stripes Forever" as the closing song of the final concert for as long as anyone can remember. After some encouragement from the band, we've decided to play the finale despite the unexpected fireworks."

The crowd cheered!

With the downstroke, the brass section played Sousa's rousing opening, followed by the woodwinds. The adrenaline was still coursing through my system as the song flew by. When Abby stood, apparently expecting to play her piccolo while buried amidst the flutes, I took my piccolo from the music stand, stepped from the podium, took her hand, and led her to the front of the stage where we waited for the beat where the piccolo solo started. We played flawlessly, and after the trill at the end of the solo I took Abby's hand. We took a bow together and accepted the rousing applause from the audience. When she went back to the flutes she was greeted with hugs and shoulder pats.

At the end of the song the band received a standing ovation as I stepped aside and joined in the applause. The ovation had been going for nearly a minute when Brian Johnson stepped forward, with his holey tuba. He took the microphone, which hushed the crowd.

"In case you didn't know, Peter 'Doc' Rogers was drafted just last week to conduct the band for the final two concerts after John Carr broke his foot. I think Peter has done an outstanding job of stepping into the job and whipping these two concerts together. Please give him a round of applause."

Brian stepped aside and started clapping and was quickly followed by the entire band and audience, who were still standing. I felt the redness creeping up my neck and looked at Dolores. She had a conspirator's grin on her face as she winked at me.

Chapter 28

The audience dispersed as the band broke down the chairs, hauling them from the stage to the bandshell basement. I got a whiff of Honey Cavendish pipe smoke as I was helping carry chairs, and found Len Rentz standing near the basement entrance.

"Good job," he said, shaking my hand.

"I'm a little relieved to have it all behind me. The last week has been nerve-wracking."

"The concert was good too," Len said, "but I was talking about taking Ashley Warren down while she was trying to shoot Sheila O'Keefe. Most people ran for cover at the sound of the gunshots. You jumped off the stage and tackled her."

"It seemed like the thing to do."

"I'm sure you're curious about Ashley," Len said, inspecting his pipe. "She's a perennial winner of the county fair quilt competition. She always gets entry to the State Fair with her quilt ribbon, so she'd already booked motel reservations in St. Paul for the entire ten days. This year she came in fourth and is ineligible for the State Fair. Ashley knows and respects Arlene Bartlett and Nancy Mohr, but Sheila O'Keefe was a new competitor and she started snooping around as soon as she saw the reserve champion ribbon on Sheila's quilt. When she found out Sheila hadn't been buying fabric at quilt shops nor had she been seen at any of the quilting groups she got suspicious. After online search for a quilt pattern featuring a bassoon, Ashley saw that a bassoon-themed quilt won the 2009 Missouri State Fair competition and it was later sold at a fund-raising auction in Branson, Missouri. It didn't take much research beyond that to find a photo of the winning Missouri quilt on the Internet and that was proof Sheila hadn't sewn the winning quilt. Ashley complained to everyone except the County Fair judges, hoping someone would catch on and turn Sheila in, without it looking like she was being a sore loser. When her subtle approach didn't work she decided to scare Sheila off or kill her."

"Ashley isn't in the band. How'd she get a peanut into Sheila's reed container on the county fair bandshell?" I asked.

"She gave a 4-H kid a buck to do it. She told him she was playing a practical joke on her friend, the bassoon player. I guess Ashley overheard Sheila turn down some nuts at a bar one night, explaining she has an allergy, and Ashley filed that tidbit away until Sheila's quilt took "her" reserve champion ribbon at the fair."

"Why would Sheila buy an award-winning quilt and enter it in the county fair competition?" I asked.

"Sheila wrote a loan for Robbie, Ashley's husband, which allowed him to quit his railroad job and open a taxidermy business. Ashely suspected there had been something going on between Robbie and Sheila, but when the business started out very slowly, and they had no health insurance, Ashley called the bank and tried to get them to restructure the loan, threatening to expose what she saw as Sheila's shady role in making the loan. In the end, there had been nothing between Sheila and Robbie, but the bank wanted to squelch any bad publicity so they rewrote the loan, at almost zero interest, and Sheila got a black mark from the bank. I guess entering the quilt in the fair was her way of getting back at Ashley, who took great pride in getting her quilt to the State Fair competition."

Noise behind us caused Len to look over my shoulder. Jeremy and Howard were lugging a stack of lawn chairs while Jeremy was chattering away about the night I'd thrown him to the floor last spring after Dolores tried to shoot a rabbit. "I'm telling you, Grandpa, it was just like that. Peter gets me on the floor and he races toward the sound of the gunfire. It's like he has a death wish or something."

The story ended just as they reached us and Jenny's dad set down his stack of chairs. He took my right hand in both his hands. "Jeremy, I'm pretty sure Peter doesn't have a death wish. He's just one of those extraordinary people who is more concerned about the safety of others than his own safety. The military pins medals on their chests and the rest of us call them heroes."

I stood there speechless, shaking hands as I broke into a sweat and flashed back to a dusty Iraq military compound. A dozen of us had been pulled forward after a flag-raising ceremony and a Marine Corps colonel was walking down the row, pinning purple hearts on our chests and shaking hands. I could feel the burning stitches that ran inside my bicep where the Iraqi bullet had grazed my arm and I could hear the flag snapping in the hot desert wind.

I was pulled away from the flashback when Jenny pushed her way between us and gave me a hug. Then I heard the clinking of bangles that always preceded my mother's arrival. Mother cut in on Jenny and hugged me while Jenny's mother, Barbara, stood aside, prim, proper, and pressed.

"Barbara called and told me you were directing the band again tonight. I'm afraid I was a little late but I saw you jump from the stage to wrestle that crazy woman to the ground and I heard the last song. I told the people standing around us that you were my son. You made me proud." In my entire life I couldn't remember my mother ever saying those words.

Ignoring Jenny, Mother linked her arm in mine and said, "C'mon, I'm buying you supper."

I stood still and she asked, "What's wrong."

"The rest of the family is joining us too." I stepped away from Mother and gave Barbara a hug, which she actually returned. I took Barbara's hand and led her to mother. "You two should get to know each other better."

"Of course we should!" Mother announced, grabbing Barbara and Jenny's hands.

Len pulled on my sleeve and in an outdoor voice asked, "When are you buying Jenny a diamond?" He pushed me toward the family before I could answer.

With my mouth agape, I found the three women staring at me. Words escaped me.

Mother, seeing the look on my face, took charge. She let go of Jenny's hand and started pulling at her chubby fingers with her right hand. After a substantial effort that garnered the attention of Jenny's entire family, she pulled a ring free.

"Here," she said, handing me a gold ring with a series of small diamonds embedded across the crest. She looked at me expectantly and finally said, "Being rather free-spirited in our youth, your father and I never had a formal engagement. We lived together while he went to law school. When we married he had a job at a law firm and we suddenly had money. He gave me this lovely ring he called my engagement ring."

I stared at the ring, having seen it on mother's finger for decades, but never really looking at it before. I looked up and saw her eyes clouded with tears. "At this point, the tradition is that you would get down on one knee..." she said before she lost her voice and flipped a hand at me, telling me to get on with it.

I turned to Jenny, who was wide-eyed and as dumbfounded as I. I looked down at my torn grass-stained pants and searched for words. I wasn't opposed to proposing to Jenny, I was just unprepared to ask her at that moment, with all of our family and others watching. For one second I had a terrible feeling of dread that she might say no.

The ring was jerked from my fingers and Jeremy turned to Jenny. "Mom, he wants you to marry him. Will you say 'yes' so we can get something to eat? I'm starving!" He lifted her left hand and jammed the ring on her middle finger where it stuck at her knuckle. As Jeremy stepped aside Jenny lifted her hand and examined the ring then looked at me with tears filling her blue eyes. I was still speechless, but I managed to nod.

Jenny slipped the ring from her middle finger and slid it on her ring finger. She stared at it for what seemed like minutes before lunging at me, nearly knocking me to the ground.

"Yes," she whispered in my ear as we hugged.

Acknowledgments

In any fictional endeavor there is the part my golfing buddy, Vern Redenbaugh, calls, "Making up stuff," where I draw inspiration from a number of sources.

As with *Whistling Pines*, I thank Brian Johnson, a resident of Two Harbors who really is a Tubist in the Two Harbors City Band, and several people he provided as contacts, who gave me great background on Two Harbors and the band. Among those contacts are: Albee who may have been lost in history, but has been revived and enhanced here. John Carr is one of the band directors and the use of him as the fictional band director is by no means meant to diminish his profound musical abilities, including being able to fill in on a number of instruments when required. I use Brian, Albee, and John as characters with my profound thanks for their input and their willingness to provide color to the story. I must add that Brian is extremely colorful in his own right, and has supplied most of the tuba jokes. Believe me, I too groaned the first time I read each of them.

Phyllis Comstock, a remarkable chemist, musician, and dear friend, was kind enough to provide her clarinetist viewpoint of the dynamics and politics of an orchestra.

The new *Whistling Pines* characters, Nancy Helmbrecht, the new director, and Barbie Burk, the expert florist in the dining room, are friends from "Dandelion Floral and Gifts," In Mora, Minnesota, who have generously supported me, and who asked to be characters in one of my books. Here you are!

Thanks to Arlene Bartlett and Nancy Mohr, quilters "extraordinaire," who helped me understand the process, time, talent, and commitment required to complete a quilt. Arlene's quilt was the grand champion at the Carlton County Fair in 2012. It was a kaleidoscope with incredible colors and patterns, all sewn together from tiny pieces of fabric with love and care. Beyond quilting, Nancy and Larry Mohr provide me with inspiration and constant encouragement.

I really couldn't have completed this book without the aid and encouragement of Frannie Brozo. It was Frannie who suggested the title *Whistling Sousa.* After reading the manuscript she told me the book left her walking the house whistling Sousa.

Thanks to editor Pat Morris who asked numerous questions about the plot, the characters, and the situations, making me think them through and re-write them until they were sharp and clean.

I have to credit my mother-in-law, Hildur Lund, my uncle Frank Hovey, my parents, George and Lorraine Hovey, and other senior citizens who provided color, smiles, and stories.

Through the efforts of one of my readers, Mike Mercer, I was introduced to retired Chief William Finney of the St. Paul Police Department. The chief provided me with incidents from his long career that had us laughing, some of which are included fictionally in this book. Thanks, Chief!

Thanks also to Dennis Arnold, who continues to provide input, color, and stories to every one of my books. He and his wife, Barb, are dear friends who helped keep our spirits up when our house in Moose Lake, Minnesota, was inundated with 3 feet of water in the "Duluth" flood of 2012.

As always, thanks to my wife Julie, who nursed me through recovery from back surgery while I wrote this book, and who is the first proofreader of each book. In her role as stoic Scandinavian, she makes sure I stay grounded and humble.

CPSIA information can be obtained
at www.ICGtesting.com
Printed in the USA
LVHW041552220119
604810LV00016B/588/P